~~THE~~ CHARLATAN

A Novel by

DAVID L. SIMMONS

The Reading Glass Books
(888) 420-3050
www.readingglassbooks.com
production@readingglassbooks.com

Table of Contents

Chapter 1: *High Hope* *1*

Chapter 2: *Preparation* *9*

Chapter 3: *Loveless* *21*

Chapter 4: *Too Great to Say No* *25*

Chapter 5: *Where is He* *37*

Chapter 6: *Footprints* *43*

Chapter 7: *Look Under the Rock* *47*

Chapter 9: *Guess Who Killed Mickey?* *61*

Chapter 10: *Watch Your Back Someone's Watching* *71*

Chapter 11: *Love Hurts in a Good Way* *83*

Chapter 12: *Julius Wilbur* *93*

Chapter 12: *Fake Alibi* *99*

Chapter 13: *The Show Must Go On* *103*

Chapter 14: *Nervous?* *107*

Chapter 15: *Anyhow, Any Way* *117*

Dedicated to Artificial Intelligence,
The Great Pretender

You are of your father the devil, and your will is to do your father's desires. He was a murderer from the beginning, and does not stand in truth, because there is no truth in him. When he lies, he speaks out of his own character, for he is a liar and the father of lies.

John 8:44

Chapter 1

High Hope

Early one evening in a bar known as Alton's Nest, The Platters' *The Great Pretender* played over speakers, *"Pretending I'm doing well."* A jazz band known as The Notes were setting up on stage. He thought, "Fedoras and sharply tailored suits mingled amongst tables. Fashion bonnets and tams matched colorful dresses as women alluringly socialized. Lavish priced shoes and heels were worn as though anything less would be half-stepping. Bartenders worked earnestly shaking and pouring drinks."

A well-dressed man, Julius Wilbur sipped cognac at a table. His mission was rogue.

One waitress said to another waitress, "He's a Candy Rapper also known as Jay Dub; short for Jay Double U(JW)."

Jay thought, "The low light was ideal for fickle characters. Their attire was that of entrepreneurs, but their conversations were like that of dealers, pimps, and prostitutes down on the corner."

Jay summoned a waitress in a scanty black dress trimmed in white. She sauntered over to him.

Jay looked up to her and said, "Have you seen Barry Johnson?"

"No, I haven't," she said as she looked down at him and continued, "Don't know what to expect from you. You come here expecting to fit in. But nobody knows you."

Jay said, "I've only been here a few times. I met Barry the other night. He told me to call him Crook. Now, my driver is waiting down the street. So, if Crook isn't here, I'll be moving on."

She said, "That don't mean squat round here. Put up or get out." She held out her hand.

"If I leave, you're gonna miss my money." He rose from the table, gave her a ten, and said, "Tell Crook, he must like not making money." He turned, and made his way through the jam-pack floor, to the entrance.

Jay walked on a sidewalk amongst Friday night bar hoopers and riff-rafts. He crossed Washington Avenue and then turned up 15th. Not far from there was a housing project called Morgan Hunt Development and next to it was The Leisure Apartment Complex. He entered The Leisure and ascended the stairs.

On his way up, he recognized one of Alton's Nest customers. Jay said, "That's right! Git it before they spend it!"

Frank Ross relaxed and said, "I thought you were going to rob me, but you're right. I have to collect." Frank knew The Leisure rent was paid uptown at the Sears building.

Jay thought it was strange, but disguised his thought with a half-smile, and said, "Catch you later." He walked up the stairs to apartment 306, unlocked the door, and went inside.

******

Penny Clark got undressed in the restroom of a modeling firm named Angels Incorporated LLC. She slipped into an evening dress, and then applied her makeup in the mirror. After which, she headed for the production floor. For as long as anyone could remember; she was never punctual.

Nowadays, Penny works as a fashion designer assistant at Angels Incorporated on the Eastside. Her dirty blond boss, Marge Gray was dressed in a plaid shirt tucked in khakis with Sperry boat shoes. She noticed Penny's talent for style and acted on it.

Marge said, "I need you to go to Clippers. Tell Warren, I want them at the Alton Arena at five sharp. I want them to style the models' hair in a way that would complement the outfits. Remember, the theme is Raging Sea."

Penny looked at her watch; 3:45pm. She had a rendezvous at 4:00. However, she couldn't say no to Marge. She grabbed her purse from the table and said, "Sure. See you tomorrow."

Penny went to Clippers down the street. Inside the hair saloon clippers buzzed, scissors snip, and shampoos were liberally applied. She approached the owner of Clippers; a pudgy man with a nappy pompadour. She said, "Warren, Marge wants you to supervise the hair styles of the models."

"What do you have in mind," asked Warren. He handed her a chart of hair designs.

She thumbed through pages with a range of styles and stopped only to point at the ones she preferred. She said, "These will do except Leola has autonomy." She walked to the door, turned, and said, "Be ready to go to work in the dressing room at Alton Arena at five next Friday." She left.

By now, Penny was running late. She boarded the subway like a salmon jumping up stream over departing passengers. The train began to move, and she began to sway back and forth until they came to the next stop. Passengers disembarked while some passengers boarded. The train pulled away slowly before it began to pick up speed. In next to no time, she was back to swaying back and forth. Before long, she got off at 15th Street. She hustled to The Leisure and ran up the stairs to Apartment 306.

******

In the meantime, Barry Crook Johnson arrived at Alton's Nest and stood at the door. His six-foot-three frame was clothed in a herringbone suit.

The Notes began to finish their rendition of the Wah effect of *Winter's Gone*. A piano player fingers brilliantly pranced over its keys. A saxophonist blew hard and strong. A lead guitarist and a cello player plucked its strings in harmony to the drummer's snazzy beat.

Crook strolled through the joint before he walked to the bar, grabbed a stool, and ordered, "Rum and coke." He spun around, sat back, and looked at the dance floor.

On stage now was Martin Sanders performing *Wanna be Loved*. He was a harsh yet tender tenor that solemnly sang, *"You too, wanna be loved."*

"Ditty bop de boo," Martin Jitterbug Sanders was into the scat verse of the song. He instantly create a melancholy presentation of the melody with scat.

A waitress walked up to Crook and said, "Jay Wilbur was looking for you. He asked are you tired of making money?"

Crook eyed her up and down.

"Don't look at me that way," She said, "That's what Julius said."

He wondered where she fit. He said, "I met him the other night. I don't know him. We just exchanged small talk. Now, where do you fit in?"

She said, "I don't have an angle. I'm just relaying the message. I don't know him either."

"Never trust a man who talks about money," said Crook. He continued, "We didn't talk about money the other night. Now all of a sudden, it's the first thing out of his mouth."

She said, "Look around. Money is all that matter. Maybe, you should hear him out."

"If he's here in the next few minutes," said Crook as he went on, "I'll listen to what he has to say."

******

Seated at a table were three dapper men. They looked at Crook as if he was their nights prey.

Dressed in a navy suit, white shirt and red necktie, Keith Star studied him. He said, "Wonder what's his weakness."

Martin Jitterbug Sanders had finished his set. He was dressed in his grey stage suit when he sat with them. He said, "The other night, I saw him talking to someone I know."

Gin German Gordon wore a brown pinstripe suit, eggshell shirt, and yellow tie. He said, "Wondered what he's up to."

Jitterbug said, "The other dude wasn't half-stepping. He wore a four Gee navy tailored suit, fifteen hundred dollars dress chukkas, and he peeled his cash from a wad."

"Was he for real?" Gin German asked.

Jitterbug said, "As real as Pam Grier."

Keith said, "Can he carry his weight?"

Jitterbug said, "Like Sampson, baby. But check it out for yourself. He just walked in."

Jay stood by the door and visually searched the club for Crook. He looked over at three dudes seated at a table. He look at a man known as Roy Clark the banker seated in a booth. He searched the bar and saw a man wave him over. It's Crook.

Crook spun to the bartender and said, "Cognac." He spun around.

Jay said, "For a while, I thought you weren't going to show."

Crook nodded and said, "A man of his word will show."

Jay said, "Let's grab a table."

Crook spun and said to the bartender, "Have the cognac brought to my table." He grabbed his drink, spun, and stood from his stool.

Jay led Crook to a table next to the three men. They sat and the waitress placed Jay's cognac in front of him.

Crook sat and said, "You mentioned money to that waitress. What's your angle? Drugs? Liquor? Women? What?" An associate told him to check him out. He may be the one.

At that moment Jay realized Crook was a crook. He said, "Completely legit. I need a businessman who can steer me in the right direction," he said, "You see, I've been asked to sponsor a fashion show and I want you to go with me."

Crook veered from Jay, looked at him, and said, "Are ya a left hand?" Crook motioned with jazz hands.

Jay laughed heartily. He said, "No. Not by a long shot. I figured if you're involved, they'll think I'm connected."

"Why me," asked Crook. "Roy Clark is right over there. He can help ya." He figured if he had to kill someone, it would be him.

Jay said, "That's where my money is coming from. Always use other people's cash."

"I see. Who's the fashion designer?"

Jay said, "Ever heard of Marge Gray? It's one of her shows."

Crook knew this guy was real. Marge Gray was huge. He said, "How did you land that?"

"You ever heard of Julius Wilbur from Atlanta with investments all down the east coast?"

Crook said, "Can't say that I have, and I know a lot of guys. But that name sounds familiar. Is he a boxer?"

"See, you don't know everybody. Julius Wilbur is me. I'm a former boxer. Some folks call me Jay Dub."

Crook had to think fast. He didn't recognize him, but he said to cover his tracks, "Sure I heard of Jay Dub. Man, it's good to meet ya."

Jay was convinced Crook was a hustler. He said, "Good to meet you. So, will you join me? I've heard the after parties are a trip. Perhaps, I can introduce you to Leola Sparke."

Crook livened up and said, "Sure, I'm in and I'll go." Then he asked, "When?"

"Next Friday," said Jay. "Be ready by six. I'll pick you up here." He stretched out his hand and they shook.

The three dapper men heard every word. They rose from their table and walked outside. It wasn't long before Jay appeared from the club. He walked up the street, looked around, and then headed toward The Leisure Apartments.

Jitterbug tailed Jay up to Washington. The other two dapper men went back inside to watch Crook. Behind them was Penny Clark; Roy Clark's sister.

Jay walked briskly. He walked into the entrance of The Leisure and went up the stairs. Jitterbug wasn't far behind. When he saw Jay enter and walk up the stairs, he knew something didn't seem right.

Chapter 2

Preparation

Monday morning, she was dressed in a black windowpane Norfolk jacket. Underneath it, she wore a white shirt, black necktie, black slacks with black wedge clogs. The dirty blond, Marge Gray walked into her office and sat behind her desk.

Marge was born Margarette Hilton Gray in Lynn, Massachusetts. Her father, Earl Gray was an engineer with a master's from MIT. Her mother, Hillary Gray was an adjunct professor at Boston College. Marge had a decent childhood and after she graduated from high school, she was accepted in the Harvard School of Business.

She did her intern at Michael Coors' Fashion. It was a nifty way to recruit undergrads for the fashion industry. Marge was a good intern in that she worked hard to learn the fashion industry. After she graduated, she convinced her father to put up the capital for her fashion business called Angel Incorporation L.L.C. These days, Marge is renowned in the fashion industry. That's where she got her second education. She was introduced into the crafty street life. After a period of time, she was stigmatized as a tough biscuit to deal with.

Marge took Penny Clark under her wings, but there was one issue; Marge was gay from her college days and Penny was straight because of the Air Force policy. That's when Cheryl showed up at Angel Inc.

The door opened and the Mirror Productions representative walked in and sat.

Marge said, "We've been working on this show for a year. I've signed fourteen models from Padfield Model Agency for sixty thousand dollars."

Janice Merlin of Mirror Productions was dressed in a cream shell with a black leather skirt. She said, "We managed to secure a venue for thirty-two thousand five hundred dollars at Alton Arena for Friday. Our slot has been on their books for a year. So, we have to make good on it."

Marge said, "Great. I agree to your firm suggested theme for the show, The Raging Sea. I notice it's heavy on the lighthouse theme. Even the food is demanding." She waved her hands as she spoke, "Lobsters, crabs, shrimp, and grilled halibut catered from Reese's Deep Sea. For that reason," said Marge, "I preferred The Fishbowl theme. It would have been cheaper. Our budget for production as of today is a firm thirty thousand dollars, which by now, every dime is accounted for."

Janice said, "As of Saturday morning, we have accumulated nine thousand dollars for the front row seating. I don't understand why they wouldn't chip in the seats. Our lighting is set at thirty thousand dollars. Mirror Productions have hired DJ Hoss, a sound engineer, for eighteen hundred dollars. We had a problem booking the rapper Cee Note. He's a fragile situation."

Marge said, "He's one of Leola's closest friends."

"May I remind you; he was acquitted for the murder of Piru." Janice looked around and then whispered, "Piru was a gangster."

Marge said, "So, no big deal. Cee Note traveled with an entourage who are stars in their own right. Stars like Knicks point guard Buddy Webb, LA rapper Sharky, and that rhythm and blues singer Antony Howell. They can draw an audience. I suggest you make it happen."

"Will do," said Janice. "But you must keep this under consideration, security will have to be beefed up. Which will put an added five thousand dollars onto the budget. As of today, seventy thousand dollars for set design is already accounted for."

Marge said, "You got it." She sat back and said, "What about the limo service?"

"Peanuts," said Janice, "We got it thru Aero Exclusive Transportation for ten thousand dollars."

Marge said, "We have spent so far two hundred, forty-eight thousand, and three hundred dollars of an eight hundred thousand dollars budget. The way it looks, it's going to take every bit of it. But we have two hundred thousand dollars in reserve. So, all we have to do is rehearse, and then execute."

"Will do, Marge," said Janice. "Will do."

******

Meanwhile, the Star brothers waited on the corner of Washington Avenue and 16th Street. That corner was called Hustler's Nibbana.

A blond, Black lady with a short haircut, Shawana Baker known as Cookie strolled up to them and asked, "You got it?"

Keith Star said, "You know I do." He reached into his coat, pulled out a sandwich bag of marijuana, and handed it to her.

She said as she paid him, "Cool." And then she yelled, "Frank!"

Frank Ross pulled up, she got into his car, and they drove off.

******

In the meantime, Crook jogged in Midway Park. He was well into his pace when Jitterbug joined him.

Jitterbug said as they jogged, "Nice day."

"That's right, huff," said Crook. "What's your angle?"

"No angle, huff, just taking in this morning air, huff," replied Jitterbug. "Saw you with that new dude Friday night, huff."

"You're talking about Jay Dub, huff," said Crook.

Jitterbug said, "Yea, that guy. Huff, huff. Is that his name?"

"Huff, he prefer to be called Jay."

Jitterbug said, "Huff, what does he do for a living?"

"He's an ex-boxer. Huff; he was the number one contender until Austin Reed landed a punch that detached his left retina. He retired from boxing and since then been making investments along the east coast."

Jitterbug stopped.

Crook stopped and said, "Are you all right? You look troubled."

"I'm all right. Just thought of something," said Jitterbug.

They resumed jogging.

Crook said, "He told me about a fashion show this Friday and want me to join him. Huff."

"Huff is he a homo," asked Jitterbug.

"No, huff, he just want people to think he's connected."

"Good luck," said Jitterbug. "Huff."

******

Jay stepped out of The Leisure and got into his Corvette. He pulled from the curb, swerved into traffic, and whipped around the corner onto Washington Boulevard with Teddy Pendergrass blasting from his sound system, *Life is a Song Worth Singing*.

He parked at a magazine stand and bought a newspaper.

The merchant said, "The Star brothers are looking for you. Cookie is looking for you too." He paused and said, "Don't know them."

Jay hopped back into his car and sped to a donut stand. He got out, pointed at a pastry, and said, "That one."

The owner said, "The Star brothers are looking for ya."

"By now, they could be at my apartment," said Jay. "But why are they looking for me?"

"Don't know bro," said the owner.

Two men across Washington Avenue watched Jay. Keith and Gary Star watched him leave the donut stand.

Keith said, "This cat must do heavy jobs for people that can't use the law." But this time, it was different. Keith and Gary hunted Jay to get answers. Keith said, "Let's go wait at his crib." They got in Keith's caddie and motored off.

Not long, off 15th street, Jay went up the stairs to his apartment. He noticed the door to his apartment was cracked. He stepped back, kicked the door, and it slammed into Keith's face. Jay curled and punched Gary in his gut. He whipped around without hesitation and threw a jab to Keith's chin.

Next, Jay spun around and whipped his leg. He caught Gary on the leg, and he crashed to the floor. He grabbed Keith and slammed his face into the wall. Jay pimped slapped Gary and searched him. He said to Keith as he walked out, "It's obvious, you don't know me."

******

Jay hit the streets with *Somebody Told Me* by Teddy Pendergrass played on his car radio. He stopped an elderly lady on the sidewalk that went by the name of Miss Mary Bee.

Jay asked, "Have you seen Cookie?"

She said, "She ain't been around here in a while."

He moved on.

Jay asked Oscar Smith from the Eastside, "Have ya seen Cookie?"

"You should know where to find her," said Oscar, "She's been looking for ya all morning."

Jay got into his car.

******

Back at Jitterbug's uptown apartment. He said, "He beat the crap out of ya'll."

Keith said, "We didn't stand a chance. He could throw punches where he wanted."

Gary added, "He knew how to use his body too."

Jitterbug said as he strolled to a window to get a view of the Lewis River. "Guess I'll have to pay Ms. Marge Gray a visit. Call Gin German."

Keith got up and walked to the phone.

******

Frank Ross was a local businessman. He owned Pigeons, a soul food restaurant in the New Hills district. When the demographics of New Hills changed to Vietnamese, his business went under, and his million dollars investment bellied up. He lost everything and now stays on 15th Street in The Leisure apartments.

Frank hung out at Alton's Nest to flaunt his wealth. These days, he hangs out there hoping no one will discover the real reason why he's always at the bar. This Monday, he waited for Cookie to score. She did. He picked her up and went to his apartment.

Cookie was a part time model. Her cupid lips, high cheek bones that ended with a vee at her chin were captivating characteristics. Her short dyed blond hair accented her cream complexion.

After high school, she enrolled in Styx Academy of Arts where she was awarded a thespian certificate. Yet it was her looks that inspired her to move forward. She went on to enroll in a traditional education school at Bennet College in Greensboro, North Carolina. There she majored in Sociology and graduated Suma Cum Lada.

After graduation, Cookie managed to hold down a few minor jobs, but her sights were set for the stage. In time, she met this humble but firm influential woman in the fashion industry. However, Cookie had her faults. Once, the first time she wore six inch heels during a show, she was reputed to have fallen on the runway. Cookie was told to practice in a mirror, but she was stubborn. So, she had to pay the tab for ignorance. Marge kept faith in her. She was hired for this show under the assumption it's going to show her value to the industry. That Monday morning, Cookie sat in Frank's apartment.

Frank said as he rolled a joint, "Did you find him?" He licked the joint up and down, and went on, "You know it's important I make contact." He handed it to her.

"No," said Cookie as she lit the joint. "It's hard to keep him on a schedule." She took a drag, held it, and then handed it back to Frank. She asked, "Why do you need him?"

Frank took a drag, held it, exhaled, and said with a smoke covered face, "I don't want him going around telling everybody I live here." He took another hit, snorted, and handed it back to Cookie.

She took it. Took another hit and held it. She exhaled. "Why would he tell them," asked Cookie with droopy eyes. "He doesn't know you that well and he doesn't know them." She relaxed in the chair and looked at Frank in a flirty way.

"I want to keep it that way," said Frank. He held out his hand, she held it, and he led her into his bedroom.

******

Eddie Grant paced angrily on the sidewalk hoping he would show. Eddie lived in the Morgan Hunt Development. That public housing had one port of call; watch your step. He hung out with other Black young men who were veterans of the juvenile dragnet. Young men who were dedicated to rob and extort rather than get a legitimate job. He worked off of hope; hope he will set things right.

It was reported that once he followed an intimidator from school, Johnny Holmes. Outside Morgan Hunt Development, Eddie approached him.

Eddie said, "Ain't so big now, are ya hot shot?"

Johnny turned and swung a powerful round house. Eddie ducked, and then sent a jab to Johnny's jaw. A crowd of teenagers surrounded them. Even his little sister who came out to greet Eddie saw him beat Johnny to the ground. Eddie beat Johnny because he mocked a disabled girl who was having a tough time carrying her books. That day, his four-year-old sister called him Gluck. Gluck was the sound Johnny made each time he was punched. Eddie never liked the nickname, but he accepted it.

Eddie was good-looking. He stood six feet, head full of hair, square jaws, and a cleft chin. He was well toned, and he stylishly wore oversized clothes. He held the impression; he was an awfully attractive thug.

Eddie's father was a truck driver and his mother worked two jobs. In spite of their income, they still couldn't get ahead. Many nights he went to Alton's Nest to supply security for cars.

Well, that particular Monday, he met up with the men who would change his life. When this man came downtown, Eddie would watch his Cadillac. They became close, but Eddie wanted the same-like possessions the man owned. On the other hand, he wasn't willing to do what it took to get it. Eddie needed a formal education. The man understood that and once explained it to him.

The man explained, "With an education, ya learn how to think like rich folks. They break laws like everybody else. So, ya learn how to break laws and get away with it. Education will show you where money flows. It's no coincidence why rich people seek counsel. Their professors recommend and steer them. Who in turn will get a piece of the action along with the school."

Eddie walked up and down the block in front of Fast Break Corner Store when a Cadillac pulled up and parked. Jitterbug rolled down the passenger window and said across Gin German, "Watch the car while we go inside."

"Sure," said Eddie. He stood erect with crossed hands.

After a brief time, Jitterbug and Gin German returned. Jitterbug handed Eddie a ten and said, "Wanna make some real money?"

"Sure, ya know I'm down," said Eddie.

Jitterbug said, "Going to see this woman who may give you a shot. Hop in."

Eddie got into the backseat. Gin German got in on the passenger side while Jitterbug slid under the steering wheel. The car started and pulled into traffic.

*****

Crook was refreshed and ready for the rest of the day. Jay picked up Crook on Washington. He took Crook to his Leisure apartment off 15ᵗʰ. The moment they walked in, Crook frowned. Stuff was thrown in many directions. He joined Jay in straightening up. Jay was meticulous. Everything had to be put back in place.

Jay said, "I recalled seeing one of the men at the bar. The other guy, I didn't know."

"Why were they here? This doesn't look like a place you would live," said Crook. "Oh, you're plastic like a lot of guys around here." He pointed and said, "You almost had me fooled."

Jay said, "Some of us are real. But, between you and me, there's a charlatan."

"I'm real as real can get," claimed Crook. "But you," he looked around and said, "might have some explaining."

Jay said, "I know I'm Jay Dub. And since you know you're Crook, we both can't be charlatans."

"No, you're missing the line of reasoning," said Crook. "Who are you?"

*****

Jitterbug, Gin German, and Eddie stood outside of Marge's office. Jitterbug said, "I want you to go in and request to the receptionist an interview with Marge for a modeling job. If she say no, just say that's ok I'll wait. We'll come in a few minutes later." Jitterbug pointed and said, "Go ahead."

Eddie went into the office. Penny was at her desk and the receptionist, Cathy said, "May I help you?"

Eddie said, "I'm Eddie Grant. I'm here for an interview with Marge Gray."

Cathy searched her appointment calendar and said, "I don't see you listed." She looked at him and noticed an eye-catching young man. She got up and said, "Please, have a seat. Wait here." She went into Marge's office.

Marge hung up the phone and went back to studying her paperwork. She then began to peck on her laptop.

Cathy walked into her office and said, "There's a young man outside who claimed he had an appointment with you."

"What's his name," asked Marge.

"Eddie Grant."

Marge said, "I can't recall his name. Is he potent, handsome?"

"Yes indeed. He's intoxicating. He's here for an interview."

Jitterbug and Gin German walked into the front office.

Penny stood but Cathy remained seated at her desk. Cathy said, "May I help you?"

Jitterbug said, "No, but Ms. Gray can."

"Do you have an appointment?"

Gin German said, "We don't need one." They went into Marge's office.

Cathy turned and said firmly, "You can't barge in here like this. Do you have an appointment?"

Jitterbug said, "Don't need one."

Marge stood and said, "Cathy, it's all right. Leave us."

Marge was a street wise gal. She knew what they wanted. This wasn't the first time this happened before a show. She said, "May I help you while at the same time you can help me?"

Gin German said, "I can help you when Cookie move from reefer to coke. I can keep the wolves at bay. You know," he paused, patted his hair, and went on, "keep them in check."

Marge laughed and said, "You're a day late and a dollar short. I've got protection. Let me see." She reached into a drawer, searched the paperwork, and then said, "Can't find some complimentary tickets, but if you stop by tomorrow, I can give you some tickets and you can see my protection. They will enjoy throwing you out as a warmup."

"Don't need your tickets," said Jitterbug. "I can guarantee we'll be close by." They turned and stormed out of her office.

Marge reached into her drawer, covered a pistol with paperwork, and closed it.

She said, "Cathy, send in Mister Grant."

Her office door opened, and he entered. He was perfect.

Eddie said, "I need work pretty bad, but I thought I'll give you the first shot."

Marge smiled and said, "That's not how it works. I can refer you to a model agency, but in the meantime, I'll hire you as my janitor. I promise to pay you generously. What do you think?"

"I'm not with sweeping floors," said Eddie. "But if that's what it takes to start a modeling career, I'm game."

Marge said, "Good, see me Wednesday at noon. Be ready to work. You may see Leola Sparke and her close friend Cee Note. Try not to lose your mind."

"You can trust me on that. See ya Wednesday and thanks for giving me a shot. Ya won't regret it."

Marge said, "No problem. I know you have what it takes."

Chapter 3

Loveless

Shawana Cookie Baker knew the streets like kids know sweets. She could out hustle any jungle bunny, yet her heart wasn't in it. She wanted to succeed, but at what? Cookie had the attributes of a fashion model and the build of a female athlete. In fact, the one thing that was held against her, she wasn't slim enough. So, she dieted and lost weight. However, she lost too much, now she's too thin by industry standards.

Her main trouble with weight loss was when she met this guy Benjamin Wright. She had seen him in the hood, but it was this particular encounter she fell for him.

Cookie was out kicking it with her female acquaintances. She met him in a corner store.

He bumped into her and said, "this is my fault. You're too beautiful to make mistakes."

She said, "Why would I want to be friends with someone as clumsy as you?"

"Ya don't halva choice," said Benjamin, "You can call the cops for a petty assault or ya can make me your man."

"You mean you're that cheap," said Cookie, "How about I treat you to lunch?"

"That'll be cool."

They dated for a while until he began to pursue a career in hip-hop. A few years ago, as his musical career grew, he was gunned down. His murder was never solved. He was a gangbanger who went by the nickname of Piru. As a result of his death, her weight peeled from her body like a banana. However, she did manage to remain competitive in the modeling profession. Frank had recovered from his setback by producing Piru. That's how he met Cookie.

Cookie rolled under the covers and said to Frank, "Where are ya gonna go tonight?"

Frank rolled to face her and said, "Comedy Form over in Jefferson Heights. They got Eric Neat performing along with local talent. Everybody's talking about it. Wanna go?"

"Well, sure," she said. "Let me sober up."

Frank said, "Okay, but why were you looking for Julius Wilbur?"

"Penny told me to look him up if I needed anything."

Frank said, "So, you're fooling around behind my back."

"Naw, baby," said Cookie. "He's trying to hit on Penny. She got the financing for the fashion show. Close to a million."

Frank sat up and said, "He's that loaded?"

"Yea, he's loaded."

"Well, why is he hanging around a dump like this," asked Frank.

"Don't know," said Cookie. "Penny got it for him. He claimed he didn't want to standout."

Frank said, "You think you can get me close to him?"

"I'll try," said Cookie. "But the deal is on you. I got my own issues."

******

Jay left his apartment and drove over to Crook's Clothing Outlet. Crook's store was on the corner of Johnson and 17th. He parked out front and went inside.

Jay approached a floor person and said, "Looking for Barry Johnson."

She pointed to the rear. Jay walked to the back of the store and saw Crook wearing glasses with a pen in one hand. In his other hand was a clipboard.

A clerk said, "Spring dress multi-print two petite, two medium, and two plus."

Crook checked off the items.

Jay said, "Guess I caught you at the wrong time."

"No, you didn't," said Crook. "Ya see, I work for a living."

"Cut the crap," said Jay. "You work for the Carinii family. This is their store and their merchandise."

Crook said, "See you been snooping around. How can I trust ya?"

"You don't have to trust me, just collaborate with me and everything will be all right."

Crook asked, "What do you want now?"

"Who is Cookie," said Jay.

"I thought you would know her. She's a model."

Jay said, "So that's why she's looking for me."

"Careful, she's a hustler," said Crook. "She'll leave ya high and dry."

Jay said, "I doubt it. So, where can I find her?"

"At the fashion show," said Crook.

Jay said, "You know what I mean. Where does she hangout and where does she live?"

"Your guess is probably better than mine," said Crook.

The clerk said, "Three distressed denim jeans, size petite and four mediums."

Crook made a couple of observations and said to Jay, "Don't sweat it. It probably nothing."

Jay said, "It may be nothing to you, but it's something to me if she's tracking me down and I don't know her."

Crook said, "Remember Jay, to have a crew, you've got to break heads."

Jay turned from him and left the store.

＊＊＊＊＊＊

Penny Willene Clark started her working career in the United States Air Force as a personnel administrator. She worked on assignments for personnel as well as duty placements. While she was on active duty, she was selected to perform in the Tops in Blue tour of the Air Force. Air Force performing personnel was quick to notice her skill in selecting outfits for her performances. As a result, others sought her advice on what to wear. The tour was a success. After a six-year commitment, she was honorably discharged.

Penny attended Winston Salem State University with a major in Visual Arts and Communication. After four years, she was awarded a Bachelor of Arts Degree in Communication. She returned to her home city and went to work for WCRF Channel 10 an affiliate of the Columbia Broadcasting System.

There she did an excellent job behind the scene. She helped with lightning, sound, and cues. Her boss was overwhelmed with the results of everything she did, he recommended her to his personal friend, Marge Gray.

Marge was quick to take her under her wings. She knew a person like Penny only comes around less than one shot in a lifetime.

Nowadays, she's Marge assistant. She's learning the trade as if Marge were grooming her to take over. It often crossed Penny's mind, why would a White woman turn her business over to a Black woman? The answer was clear and simple; Penny's talent for the model industry was impeccable, and that Penny has a jump on the competition. She has a brother who is a high-level banking official at one of the largest banks in the city, Morgan and Pearce Business Financial.

Chapter 4

Too Great to Say No

Four years earlier, a young Black man stepped onto the sidewalk from Middle Street Liquor Store over on 18th Street. He had bought a pack of Newport and a fifth of Puerto Rica rum. He walked to his black Honda Accord he had parked about four spaces down from the store.

Across the street, a young Black man noticed a black man in a car. He walked up the sidewalk, passed a taxi stand, and entered Joey Donte's Men Fine Wear.

The dude in the car saw the man with a bottle of rum and noticed he was without protection. He pulled a skull cap down over his face. He jacked a round into his pistol. In next to no time, his tires screamed from the curb.

The young man with the rum looked at the speeding car as it fishtailed towards him. He raced to his car, opened the passenger door, and threw the rum into the car. He reached for a pistol concealed in his back.

The speeding car stopped. The dude got out and fired seven shots at him. Bullets ripped and whipped his body before he flopped to the pavement. The shooter jumped back into his car and sped off.

A drive by was an everyday occurrence. Though, this hit may not be a result of a territory dispute. The man killed was a young man who had started his hip-hop career at By Gone Expressions. That made some young Black men peddlers of envy. The man name was Piru, a gangster. A gang refuse to take responsibility for a low level hit like that. Therefore, they navigated law enforcement officers to check out the music industry.

Mound Records was heavy on rhythm and blues. The label produced solid financial reports that most producers Googled. The label officials thought it would be foolish to take responsibility, but Artistic Records was another story, and their story was thought-provoking.

Artistic claimed all of their artist were accounted for, except for one.

Their official said, "He was at home, but there's no one to vouch for him because he was alone."

That artist met the description of the shooter. However, He wasn't a gangbanger, and he was considered soft.

Before long, a grand jury was formed, and the prosecutor presented its case. They claimed even though they didn't have a smoking gun, they had a credible witness. Two indictments were issued. One for the accused shooter and one for the accused driver.

In Court, the prosecutor called the credible witness to the stand. The witness was a Pakistani liquor store clerk, and he was vigorously examined by the prosecutor.

The prosecutor asked, "What did this shooter looked like?"

The witness looked at the defense table and began to describe the seated young men. "I didn't see a driver in the car, but the shooter looked about six three."

"Did either man have a beard?" Asked the Prosecutor.

"No," said the clerk. "He looked like the man seated over there." The Pakistani clerk pointed.

The Defense crossed examined the clerk and asked one question, "How can you say the shooter looked like him if the shooter was wearing a skull cap over his face? He's even wearing a beard for Christ sake."

After a lengthy deliberation, the accused shooter and accused driver were acquitted of Piru's murder.

On this day, Cee Note understood what it's like to be a household name. He was six feet three inches and weight one sixty with muscular ability to hold his place. He thought of envious people in the Black community as crabs in a barrel.

To counter the act of charlatans, Cee Note would ask, "How many Elvis records do you own?" He couldn't find one person in his community who had one Elvis record. Cee Note appealed, "But that didn't stop Elvis from becoming rich."

Cee Note's dedication and commitment to his music yielded him a fortune.

******

Janice Merlin and Leola traveled to Cee Note's mansion in The Fosters. Janice paid the toll and crossed onto Hampton Island. The Fosters was an affluent community that guaranteed privacy. There was only one way in and one way out; the toll bridge.

Janice drove to a gate that opened automatically. She drove up a winding concrete throughfare shaded by colossal oaks. The car parked in the horseshoe at the front of a Spanish tile roof mansion. The manicured lawn was a testimony of prosperity. Janice got out and followed Leola to the front door.

Leola didn't knock; the front door opened.

A full-size Black man stood at the door and said, "Come in Ms. Sparke."

They walked through a high ceiling foyer and entered the living room. It was humongous. Over-sized sofa in front of a gigantic fireplace. Bookshelves covered the walls from the ceiling to the floor with oil paintings hung between them. Janice and Leola followed the man into a den.

The man said, "Wait here." He walked over to Cee Note seated on a love seat between two sofas watching The Fugitive on television.

He said, "Ms. Leola and another lady is here to see you."

Cee Note said, "Bring 'em over."

The man ushered the ladies over to a sofa.

Cee Note stood from the love seat and gave Leola a grateful hug. He looked at Janice, nodded, and said, "Glad you could make it."

"My pleasure," Leola said and sat.

Cee Note said, "Now, what's on your mind?"

Janice said, "It's about the fashion show. Have you made up your mind?"

Leola added, "Will you do that for me?"

Cee Note thought about the business aspect and said, "My usual fee is one point two mill for a venue like that. But since Leola will be there, I'll charge what you are paying her."

Janice was lost for words. She said, "You'll do that for Leola?"

"Anything for my baby. I told her I'll be there," said Cee Note.

Janice reached into her purse, grabbed an envelope, and said, "Here's a check for one hundred and fifty thousand for twenty minutes." Leola had discussed the fee, but she didn't know Janice had another check for two hundred thousand. Just in case Cee Note refused the first offer.

Cee Note took the check, handed it to the huge man and said, "Will, take care of this."

Janice said, "Your rehearsal will be on Wednesday at 11:00. Can you make it?"

"I'll be there," said Cee Note. "If my baby is there."

Leola said, "Oh sugar, I'll make it."

Cee Note rose from the love seat and followed Janice to the front door.

Janice turned and said, "Thanks."

"Ya got it," Cee Note said as he stood and watched her get into her car and drive off.

******

Next day Tuesday, Jay had more questions than answers. He was on his way looking for a lady named Cookie. He closed his apartment door and noticed a young lady coming out of one of his neighbor's apartment. She was a short haired Black blond; built like any man preferred with a stare that would rob any thief.

Frank leaned outside the door and said, "Cookie, don't forget."

"I won't," she replied. She walked to the stairs and was intercepted by a man.

He said, "Heard you've been looking for me."

"Who the hell are you?"

"Jay Wilbur, and you're Cookie?"

Cookie veered from him, looked around and said, "Is there a place we can talk?"

"Look, I don't deal with people who are strung out," said Jay.

"I'm not strung out and I want you to listen to me."

Jay said, "I'm listening. Go ahead."

"Frank doesn't want you to let the people at Alton's Nest know he lives here."

Jay thought for a second and said, "Why would I do that when I don't even know who you're talking about."

"Don't go blabbing you mouth. Ya dig?"

Jay asked, "Who are you? My wife? Well, I'm not married, and you got the wrong guy."

"Oh, I've got the right guy," said Cookie. "Penny told me all about you." She gave him a peck on his cheek, turned, and descended the stairs.

******

Wednesday morning Penny knocked. Jay opened his door. She was taken by his appearance; pajamas and slippers. She said, "See you're ready for work."

Jay was groggy. He said, "What time is it?"

"Time for you to be ready," said Penny.

Jay said, "Producers move as they please. I've got to catch a flight to Florida later on."

"Not our producers. We got to get the kinks out. Don't cha wanna get paid?"

Jay said, "All right. Let me get dressed."

Jay and Penny got into her car. She pulled from the curb and in no time roadhouses and businesses were a blur. She said, "You seem like you're slumming."

"Why do you say that?"

She said, "Men like you can have someone else do the foot work."

"I wanted to do a hands on," said Jay. "Can't trust the loss of any more money. Been bit by that dog before."

"I see," said Penny. "Why not let someone else chase the dog?"

"Can I ask you something," asked Jay.

She said, "Sure, go ahead."

"Who told Marge about Mickey? We're a private investment firm."

She said, "Marge met him at a MET Ball show. He gave her his number and he answered."

"No fooling around?"

She said, "It was all above the table. Really, so why are you here?"

"Okay, I'm looking for someone."

She said, "Who?"

"That's for me to know," said Jay. "After we finish at the rehearsal, take me to the airport."

******

Later Wednesday morning, a limousine pulled to the curb at Weekes Bishop College auditorium. Inside, a makeshift dressing room was set up that led to a makeshift catwalk. Leola walked in with her entourage. She was followed by Cookie and other models.

A dressed smartly Black man appeared at the door. Patrick Pat Needles, a hair stylist assistant entered. Pat Needles was a second lieutenant in the United States air Force. He was stationed at Loring

Air Force Base in Maine. Not much of his background floated to the surface. Yet, he was known as the savior.

One night after shift change, gunfire was heard off of the Weapon Storage Area perimeter. A recall of Security forces was started. Lt. Needles briefed the commander and took control. The responded forces sat on a bus. Lt. Needles stepped aboard. He briefed the forces, "Shots have been reported on the perimeter. We're going to deploy on the southern perimeter of the WSA. We'll bound to get the unidentified force away from the WSA. Remember, there're friendly forces on scene. Recognize your target first before you fire."

An Airman whispered in his ear. Lt. Needles said, "The situation has been stopped. It was an off duty cop that fire his rifle in distress."

Not long afterward, he was dishonorably discharged. Why? He was fingered with an airman in a downtown club popular with gay people. Behind him was the clothes stylist supervisor, Samuel Lovey.

Samuel Lovey was an obnoxious, subtle man. He too was a security specialist in the United States Air Force. However, his story is different.

Technical Sergeant Lovey was stationed at Royal Air Force Base Alconbury in the United Kingdom. While there, he was the assistant flight sergeant for the Ground Launch Cruise Missile System forces at RAF Molesworth. His duties were cut short by Alconbury because there was the disbursal side and the base side on Molesworth. Since he was the assistant flight sergeant, he had to report for duty on the Molesworth base side. Well, his story goes like this. On Mother's Day, May 9, 1988, he held a guardmount at the base.

After the formation was dismissed, he returned to the control center to be briefed on the weekly anticipations. He was inside the center.

Airman Neal burst in and said, "Sergeant Lovey, someone is sick in the restroom!"

Sergeant Lovey stepped into the restroom. He noticed brain and skull fragments spread across the floor. The spread came from a stall. He thought, "There's no way I was gonna look in that stall."

To make a long story short, he managed the situation with extraordinary precision. Lovey's commander said, "He think so fast, his body has to catch up with him."

Later, at the end of the gulf war, he completed the four phases of alcoholism in the Social Action program. He's considered Marge's right hand man and the choir director for the 1st Baptist Church on Harlow Drive. He also like to direct movies. He was labeled The B-Movie Director. Behind him was Cheryl Ann Mann, the Model supervisor.

Cheryl Ann Mann was an Airman in the United States Air Force during the late eighties. Airman Mann was stationed at Carswell Air Force Base in Ft Worth, Texas as a Security specialist. She took part in two specific incidents.

The first incident involved alcohol. She was eighteen years old, and it was illegal for her to drink any alcohol. Well, the story goes like this. Other airmen were having a party in the dorm. Whenever an airman arrived, an airman yelled, "The Beer is in the fridge."

Cheryl named was dropped as one of the participants. Now her flight sergeant was a reasonable man. He studied the report and concluded she wasn't there. He convinced the commander of her absence, and she was let off. It should be noted, she was cited with a Driving Under the Influence a month later. The second incident was considered more severe at the time.

One evening a female airman knocked on her dorm room door. Cheryl answered wrapped in a blanket. The airman looked passed her and saw a nude female airman uncovered on a bed.

The airman said, "Be on time for training tomorrow." She turned and left. She went to the Office of Special Investigations and reported what she saw.

Cheryl and her partner were relieved of duty. Yet, a strange thing happened. The female squadron commander gave them a general discharge, which would be upgraded to an honorable discharge in six months. It happened; the commander was a lover of women. Nowadays, Cheryl Mann works for Marge's fashion firm.

Cheryl was followed by photographers.

The models began to take their seats with hair stylist positioned behind them. Pat needles ordered, "Ladies, today your hair will be set and prep for Friday."

Hair stylists began to pull, comb, and brush hair.

Leola opened a magazine while her stylist groomed her. A photographer noticed her and began to take pictures.

Sam Lovely said, "Brad, honey put on a bibb for Christ sake. Ya slavering all over your shirt!"

Models laughed as a butch dressed Marge entered the dressing room. Cheryl stepped to her and said, "Darling, they're getting ready."

Marge said, "Ladies, may I have your attention. Today we're going to get the kinks out. So, do your best work. Leola, give them tips on how to walk, pivot, and exit the catwalk."

Leola said, "Will do. But where's the fruit for today?"

"It's on the way," said Marge.

Eddie Grant swept the floor. He noticed the chemistry of the participants exercised in preparation of the show. Also, between two male models, there was an empty barber chair.

Cheryl whispered to Marge, "We have a problem. Our male model, Niger Beau Man broke his leg at the gym this morning."

"Wait here," said Marge. She walked over to Eddie and said, "Put that broom down and climb into that chair." She pointed. "I want you to pay attention because you're going to fill in for one of our models. We'll discuss the fee after rehearsal." Marge walked back to Cheryl.

******

Jay and Crook entered. They took a seat at the end of the catwalk.

Jay said, "Penny told me they needed an audience."

"They gonna need more than that," said Crook.

Frank walked in and sat opposite Jay and Crook.

Jay said, "Why are you here?"

"Special effects," said Frank. "I'm supposed to meet with the special effects technician."

"Okay," said Jay. "Y'all planning on putting on a real show."

Crook said, "Looks like I'm gonna get my money worth. Cool."

******

A limo pulled to the curb outside and Will got out to open the rear passenger door. Cee Note leaned out of the vehicle and straightened up.

Inside the dressing room, Cookie said to Leola, "How are we supposed to strut?"

"Walk like ya don't have a care in the world. Don't look anyone in the eyes, but you don't ignore them."

Cookie said, "What if you have hips like mine?"

Pat Needles said, "Child, hips like yours will stop a city bus."

The room burst into laughter. Cee Note entered with Will behind him. All eyes followed him to Leola. He leaned forward and kissed her. A kiss that threw the other models into daydreams.

Leola said, "Thanks for showing up. Don't know what I would do without you."

Samuel said, "Girl, you must be in sad shape. You're making Jesus curse."

Pat added, "Ain't no man worth it. Honey, you better come on in."

Cee Note said, "Let me go check with DJ Hoss."

******

A hip looking dude appeared at the door. A crooked fitted ball cap above the oversized shirt and baggy sagging jeans were short of gangster. DJ Hoss entered at a door at the end of the catwalk.

His assistant wheeled in two huge JBL speakers and placed them on each side of the catwalk. DJ Hoss set up two Audio-Technica turntables and hooked up wires from his station to two speakers at the end of the catwalk.

Hoss said over a mike, "Testing, one two three. Assessing one two three."

Cee Note walked up to him and said, "Loud and clear. What's up brother man?" Will stood off to the side with his hands crossed.

They fist bump and Hoss said, "Just slamming it."

Cee Note said, "I got this tune I want to use."

"Whatta ya call it?"

Cee Note said, "So Fine." He handed Hoss a CD.

Hoss put the CD into a player, put on earphones, and before too long his head began to bounce. He pulled the earphones down and said, "Man, that's straight. Have you released it?"

Cee Note said, "The fashion show will be its debut."

******

Inside the dressing room, Marge addressed the models. Marge said, "Remember we have four sets. The first set is bedroom attire. The second set is play or exercise, the third set is casual afternoon attire, and the fourth is evening formal attire. Please keep this in mind. Work on your personality for each set."

Leola said, "Gotcha."

Marge said, "Cookie, you're first up."

At the catwalk, music began to slowly come into existence. A trumpet played a solo so low it was as though a person had awakened. Cookie walked out and began to strut down the catwalk. She reached the end, looked at Frank, pivoted, looked at Jay and Crook, and then strutted back down the catwalk.

Jay whispered to Crook, "She has the right attitude."

"Yeah, I can wake up to that," said Crook.

Leola passed Cookie and sexually strutted up the catwalk. When she got to the end, she seductively looked at Frank, pivoted, and threw her buttock at Jay and Crook. She then threw her head back.

Sam shouted with joy, "That's right. Strut you dirty little heifer!"

Crook whispered to Jay, "Good Laud."

The rehearsal went through three sets. Cookie strutted gracefully down the catwalk to start the formal set. Other models followed and lined the catwalk. Leola was the final model. She was accompanied by Cee Note. The introduction to his song started before the song went into the beginning.

Chapter 5

Where is He

Last week, Mickey King was an evenhanded man. A self-made real estate mogul, he had a way of making money where most real estate investors lost. And His greatest deal was in Manhattan. He bought two buildings next to his parking garage. And then he sold them that yielded a triple profit.

Once the mob tried to muscle in on his store on 5th Avenue. He said, "No."

The men left. That night, his store was bombed. At the same time that night, the men's boss was riddled with bullets in Bensonhurst. From that day forward, he was never bothered again. He was named *The Rider without a Stallion.*

But last week, he was perplexed. How can one man lose five million dollars? Mickey was too old to track anyone down. If he were in his youth, he would have did it. Now, wealthy, and wise, he could rely on other measures. On this particular case, one of his colleagues offered to get involve. He too had lost money.

This was a sensitive situation. Contract killings was not their thing. King and Associates wanted their money back, or at least, their profits. There couldn't be any other way. First, he had to be found, and then find out his worth. Perhaps he stole the money. Either way, they're going to set things straight.

Now, Mickey had a contact in the city. He instructed his colleague to get in contact with him. The man could function as his guide in that cutthroat world.

Mickey's phone rang. He answered, "Speak."

"Yeah, can't find the charlatan. He must have skipped town." It was a lie. He knew who the charlatan was because he gave the money to him.

Mickey said, "Hold tight. I'm sending someone to help you."

"What's he like?"

"He's judicious. Careful not to overreact. Want you to show him the leads."

"Will do," he hung up.

Mickey's butler, Nadal walked into the den. "Mr. Wilbur is here."

"Send him in."

Jay Wilbur entered the den. He said, "Thanks for giving me the job. I feel it's in our best interest that I personally take this matter."

"Just got off the phone with your contact," said Mickey. "He'll show you the leads."

"What's his name?"

"Barry Johnson."

That's how Jay met Barry Johnson.

******

A while ago, most of the models wondered who was Cookie's man? Cookie was a reserved person, yet a clue existed. A local businessman picked her up after each session. The models had seen him in the newspapers and on television. He was handsome, arrogant, and witty. However, Cookie never spoke of him.

Piru said to him, "Wanna make a ton of money? Produce this record."

"Why," asked the man. "I have enough dough. Besides, if I need more money, I'll produce myself."

"Naw pops," said Piru. "That's not how it works."

The man said, "How does it work?"

"Front me and I'll make you a millionaire."

The man said, "Let me think on it."

"Don't take too long," said Piru. "I've got dawgs waiting."

He decided to take Piru up on his offer.

The man had a penthouse in Manhattan overlooking Central Park. Most of his money was invested in real estate, but he kept a few spare coins for local businesses. He opened a soul food restaurant to cover any bad money flow. Everything was groovy until a Vietnamese open a restaurant a couple of doors down. Soon, Vietnamese people began to show up in numbers. His soul food business slowed to a halt. The man thought about Piru's offer. He had to make good on the lost revenue.

Finally, things fell through. The man was ruined through gentrification. He had no way to explain how he went broke.

Piru's record landed #3 on the Billboard chart for rhythm and blues. Once again, Frank Ross had a chance at sailing high in money. At least for now, he could face the guys at Alton's Nest.

******

Wednesday afternoon after rehearsal in Marge's office.

"Real people have problems. Fake people create circumstances," Mickey said over the phone.

Marge hung up. *Tell Me Lies* by Fleetwood Mac played over the intercom.

Cheryl walked into the office and said, "It appears we still have knots. So, how do we continue?"

Marge said, "Whether things are running smooth or not, something is developing. For example, that firecracker burst that simulated special effects. I didn't intend on it to be so loud."

"I thought you approve it."

Marge said, "I didn't, but Cookie convince me to put it in the show."

Cheryl turned and said, "That's funny, I thought you were in charge." She walked out of the office. At that time, Marge didn't care about nothing. However, Cheryl didn't know why; yet she loved Marge.

******

Later that Wednesday afternoon, Cee Note was in his studio on the board when Will walked in. Baby Ray Byrd was on the microphone in the soundproof cubical. The introduction to the third song on Ray's track sounded like a train wreck until it blended into a mellow melody.

Baby Ray sang, "Gone over to my memory. Gone over to my forgot."

Cee Note cut off the mike on the board to his studio. He looked at Will and said, "What is it?"

Will nodded toward Baby Ray and said, "It's him. He's telling dudes, he killed Piru. The worst part is, he's expecting you to get him out of it."

Cee Note said, "He thinks I need him more than he needs me. Don't cha worry. I'll find a way to get him back on track. Give this to Keith. Baby Ray has got to understand…"

******

That Wednesday afternoon, Crook bought a cigar and shoved it into his pocket. One of his associates, Jitterbug bought a bag of chips. When they turned to leave, Jitterbug said, "Heard Baby Ray shot Piru."

Crook said, "And you believed it. No one talks about murder if they did it. Maybe you should see who he's protecting. He's trying to send the cops to a dead end."

Jitterbug said, "Don't think so. He's trying to get credibility for his songs."

"What he needs to do is admit he didn't kill Piru."

Jitterbug said, "How does he walk it back? We'll see."

Crook said, "Tell his fans he's for real and not a counterfeit."

Baby Ray was dog-tired. He had completed eight songs, but Cee Note persisted he stay until everything was right. Finally, after five hours, Cee Note gave his go-aheads.

Baby Ray got into his sports car and left the mansion. He had promised a young lady he would meet her at a bar. Keith waited outside the mansion on Riddles Row. When he saw Baby Ray's car, he pulled behind him.

******

Jitterbug waited at the corner of Marque and Riddles. When he saw Baby Ray's Porsche, he pulled in between Baby Ray's car and a car behind him. Jitterbug followed Baby Ray to a bar called NOTES on 23rd. Baby Ray parked on the curb, got out, and walked towards the door.

Jitterbug got out of his car, walked up to Baby Ray and said, "This is for Piru." He sucker punched Baby Ray. Baby Ray fell to the pavement. Jitterbug kicked him repeatedly. In the meantime, from his car, Keith looked at the ghastly beating.

Jitterbug said to Baby Ray, "Your days are up. I'm not through with you." Jitterbug turned, got into his car, and drove off.

Keith was satisfied. He drove from the scene.

******

Wednesday Morning, Cookie dropped Frank off at Joey's Donte's on 18th that was between Alberto's Design Jewelry and Yellow Cab Station. Even if Frank had lost his businesses due to Vietnamese gentrification, she could tell something else bothered him. Why would he go uptown? The only thing she could think of was his reputation. Frank needed clothes to receive the respect he deserved. He waved as she drove off.

Chapter 6

Footprints

Up till now, and after talking to Mickey, Jay arrived in the city. Jay invested in Marge's fashion show. Penny is his escort to show him around the city. Jay got an apartment in The Leisure. He met Barry Crook Johnson and got him interested in an investment. Jay ran into Frank Ross at The Leisure and tracked down the model named Cookie. However, he had failed to find a suspect for the charlatan.

******

That Wednesday afternoon, Mickey sank a putt on the 14th green. He mounted his golf cart and traveled to the 15th hole. 750 ft was on the sign from the 15th green with a par four. A cart pulled up behind him.

Mickey said, "I won't be long. We've got a meeting after this." He selected his club, positioned his tee, and placed his ball on it. After a couple of practice swings, he executed a perfect swing. The golf ball took off and sailed to where he wanted it to land.

The golfer in the second golf cart pulled a pistol and fired to the back of Mickey's head. Mickey's body flopped to the ground. He stood over Mickey and pumped two more bullets into his body. He went to his cart and traveled to the 16th hole.

******

Late Wednesday afternoon, the grounds keeper for Andy Hicks Golf Course finished filling the wedge marks with sand on the 14th green. He got back onto his cart. As he approached the 15th green, he thought he witnessed a body on the ground at the tee. The closer he got; he realized he was right. He raced back to the office.

About an hour later, homicide investigators arrive. Andy Hicks Golf Course was closed for the day. The 15th green was roped off with DO NOT CROSS POLICE tape. The lead investigator visionally examined the body. One shot to the head and two shots to the body. Second shot was to the middle of the back. The third shot was to the back of his throat. Three shells were collected and bagged.

The lead investigator walked into The Golf Shop. He said to the clerk, "Can I see your roster?"

"Sure," the clerk said as he spun the registration roster around.

The investigator asked, "You have an idea who did this?"

"No. We get locals and visitors all the time."

"Who was here that you didn't recognize," asked the investigator.

"There was this guy I had seen here before, but it has been a long time."

"Can I review your video?"

"Sure," said the clerk. "Follow me."

******

Jay's phone rang. He answered, "Hello."

"They got him," said the caller.

Jay asked, "What are you talking about?"

"They got to Mickey. He's gone."

Jay said, "What's going on? I just got back from Florida this afternoon. I briefed Mickey Tuesday. I came here to find the charlatan and you're telling me now I'm on my own."

"That's right pal," said the caller. "You're in the middle of a serious job."

Jay said, "Mickey was a likeable guy. Who would want to kill him, except losing five million is enough to get anybody killed."

"A lot of guys like you wanted to take his place," said the caller. "You're better off finishing what you started there."

Jay said, "I'll finish this case, but how I can do it without Mickey? I don't have a clue."

"If he told you to lookup his contact and you followed through, then you're in good shape."

Jay said, "I found his contact and is in the mix, but I still haven't found the charlatan."

"Keep looking," said the caller. "He's probably right under your nose."

"I don't think Crook is the charlatan," said Jay. "But I believe he knows him."

"When is the show?"

Jay said, "Friday evening. Everything seems to be going smoothly. I'll find him."

"Ernie Doons had an eye for Mickey's slot, but he doesn't have a crew to take care of it. Caesar Carinii is a good bet. He has an army, but why on the golf course?"

"Doons is nothing but a hustler," said Jay. "Was he there?"

"Don't know," said the caller. "I'll check him out and get back with ya. As for Carinii, he was out of town and his muscles were with him. That leaves you. You were in Florida the day he was killed. By the way, if that's the case, can you bump me up?"

"Okay, only if I get your vote," said Jay. "Keep me in the know." He hung up.

It was late Wednesday evening when Jay went to a restaurant called Phifer's known for aged steak in the third borough. He had arranged a meeting with Crook where Alton's Nest customers were unlikely to show up. He viewed the menu and ordered a cognac.

It wasn't long before Crook entered. He walked to the table and sat. The menu covered his face when Crook said, "Porterhouse steak with mushroom rue. And how about a gin and tonic."

"Glad you showed," said Jay. "I'm hungry." He waved the server over and whispered in his ear. The server nodded, made an about face, and went to the bar.

Keith and Gin German walked in. Keith looked around in search of Crook. When he turned to Gin German, he looked passed him and saw a police cruiser pull to the curb and park outside. He said, "Let's go. Now isn't the time." They turned and left.

Chapter 7

Look Under the Rock

Late Wednesday evening, Crook parked on the side of Alton's Nest on Russell Avenue and walked around to the entrance. He took a seat at the bar and ordered, "Rum and Coke."

Keith and Gin German entered. They took a seat at the far end of the bar down from Crook. Although, Keith ordered drinks, his eyes never faltered from Crook.

Frank strolled into the bar. He took a table close to the door. Before Frank sat, he noticed Keith's stare at someone seated at the bar. His eyes followed Keith eyes and their vision rested on Crook.

Now, Frank knew Crook and he knew Keith was a member of Cee Note's crew. However, he didn't understand how Cee Note would get involved. He said to the server as he sat, "Thugs. They all act the same way."

The server said, "What do you mean? Aren't they all fake?"

"No," said Frank. "They're chasing the same dime."

The server said, "Oh, you're talking about those folks. Darling, you date a fashion model." She looked at Cookie when she entered and sat. "Darling, may I take your order?"

The server listened and said, "Ya got it Babe," however before she turned around. She asked Frank, "Why are ya looking over there? Do ya like him?"

"No," said Frank, "but I find it's strange to see that guy checking out Crook."

Crook separated some dollar bills from a roll and paid the bartender. He stood and walked towards the entrance. At the same time, Keith and Gin German stood from their seats. They looked around, and then followed Crook.

Frank said, "Something don't look right."

Keith and Gin German walked out of the club as Jay walked in and tapped Frank on his shoulder.

Frank spun around and said, "Jay."

Jay said to Cookie as she got up to leave, "How are ya?"

She nodded as she answered, "Fine." She looked at Frank and said, "Going to PALMER'S."

Frank said, "Catch ya later." He looked at Jay. "Have a seat." He pointed at a chair and continued, "What do you think of Keith checking out Crook?"

Jay said, "Heard my close friend was killed in Florida. So, Keith checking out Crook is the least of my priorities."

"Why would Cee Note be interested in Crook?"

Jay said to the server, "Cognac." He looked at Frank and said, "It sounds like you're more interested in them than a date."

Frank said, "It looks like somebody is gonna get crunched."

"Crook can take care of himself," said Jay.

The server placed a napkin in front Jay and placed a drink on the table.

Jay said, "Thanks."

Frank said to Jay curtly, "You're an ass hole."

"Most wealthy people are," said Jay. "You should know that."

******

Jitterbug was an outstanding performer, but he was an unstable gangster. The streets was all he knew until he got a break in the music industry. Before his fame, he dropped out of school when he was 16 years old. From there, he started a life of unlawfulness.

It was rumored that he robbed the Morgan and Pearce Bank. Jitterbug walked in, shot a security guard, went to the first tailor, Carrol Rye, and said, "It's not your money so give me those stacks."

She obeyed but placed a dye pack in the bag.

"I hope you didn't taint the bag cause I know where you live." And he did.

She reached into the bag, grabbed the dye pack, look at him and said, "When are you going to turn me on?"

The bottom of his mask curled. He left with fifty thousand dollars and was never caught. Six months later, Carrol got a call.

She answered, "No pay; no play."

"You're serious," said Jitterbug.

To make a long story short, they dated, and he screwed her, and then gave her an expensive diamond necklace. She never reported it to the bank.

It was late Wednesday evening when Jitterbug waited for Crook on Russell Avenue. Since Crook didn't show, he drove to Palmer's. A nightclub on the lower Eastside.

******

Crook saw Jitterbug's car pull from the curb. He got into his car, started it, and drove off. When Keith saw Crook's car pull from the curb, he tapped Gin German. They went back into the club.

******

Keith and Gin German entered the club. Frank noticed them. Keith sat at a table across from them. Frank noticed Keith eyes were glued on Jay.

Frank said to Jay, "Why is that guy staring at you?"

"Don't know and I don't care. It's a free country. He can look at anything he wants."

Frank knew Jay had been hanging with Crook. Perhaps, They did a job together and Keith is pissed about it.

Frank asked, "What you and Crook got going?"

"Why you want to know? It has nothing to do with you."

******

Inside Palmer's, Jitterbug's legs went wild on the dance floor. His dance partner, Cookie spun around, bowed, and began to whip her hips. Jitterbug gripped her waist and rolled his hips. When the song ended, they retreated to his booth.

Cookie sat down and said, "Wow, that dance was crazy fun."

Jitterbug said, "Do you come here a lot?"

"Not really," said Cookie. "Too busy working. But I've seen you at Alton's."

Jitterbug said, "I thought I recognized you. You hang around with that businessman."

"Don't wanna talk about him," said Cookie. "What do you do?"

Jitterbug said, "I break legs."

Cookie rose from the booth.

Jitterbug grabbed her wrist and said, "Don't leave. It's not that bad. You're not in any danger. Break legs is a term used in the entertainment world for Break a leg, but in the security guard world, they say break legs."

She sat and said, "I knew you were Martin Sanders, the singer. Why did you say you were a security guard? You had me going."

"Just trying to have a little fun."

She said, "That's too much fun for me."

"Whatcha doing tomorrow night?"

She said, "I'll be working."

"Well," he said, "Whatcha doing after work."

"Going home and get some rest."

"Wish I could rest with ya," he said.

She said, "If you play your cards right, you can rest with me tonight.

Crook strolled into the club. He looked for Jitterbug and spotted him in a booth with a model.

******

Wednesday evening at an hour before midnight, Marge and Cheryl were cuddled in bed when The Eagles' *I Can't Tell You Why* played on Marge's audio system. Marge got up, wrapped a sheet around her body, and walked to the champagne bucket. She asked Cheryl, "Did you answer the MET Ball invitations?" She poured a glass of champagne and said over her shoulder, "Want some?"

Cheryl rolled on the bed and said, "What champagne?"

Marge said with laughter, "Are you still Horney?"

Cheryl laughed and said, "Yeah, and yes I responded to the invitations, and I don't want any champagne. I'm fine."

"Yes you are," said Marge. She walked back to the bed and stood. The sheet dropped to the floor. She got into bed and wrapped her arms around Cheryl.

Cheryl said softly, "Why did you want Cookie in the show?"

"Well, a fashion show to me is entertainment," said Marge. "All shows have scenes, and those scenes have conflict. So, Cookie is the conflict to Leola."

Cheryl said, "I did notice during rehearsal, Cookie and Leola seem to be in competition."

"They were competing," said Marge. "I was expecting that. What I didn't expect was the special effect. I wondered where they found that guy?"

Cheryl said, "They found him on the recommendation of Cookie."

"What," said Marge. "They should have come to me first. Why didn't you tell me?"

"Thought you knew," said Cheryl. "Anyway, I'm telling you now. Don't worry, it's going to be fine." She kissed Marge and rolled on top of her for another sweet release.

The Eagles crooned through the audio system, "I can't tell you why." The medley eased into a lead guitar solo to end the song.

Chapter 8 Between The Streets

In the wee hours on Thursday, Jay and Penny left Alton's Nest in his corvette.

Jay said as he navigated traffic, "At first I suspected Crook as the charlatan because, according to Mickey, Crook was the one who picked up the money. But after tonight, I don't think he's the one. Yesterday, I briefed the shareholders and boarded the first plane back. Yet here, Crook is riding high in cash. The other day, I traced his money and found out it had come from his clothing store."

She said, "Is that why you went to Florida yesterday?"

"Yes, I went there for a shareholders meeting."

Penny said as Jay unlocked his apartment front door, "Who else do you suspect is the charlatan?"

"Jitterbug," said Jay. "He worked over Baby Ray under suspicion he killed Piru. That could be why he and Crook are acquainted. Now, according to Crook, Keith and Gin German are keeping him under surveillance. Why? What will they gain from it."

Penny and Jay went into his apartment and moseyed to the bedroom. They began to get undress.

Penny said as she unzipped her skirt, "They could be covering their tracks."

"I could be a person of interest," said Jay as he unbuttoned his shirt.

Penny said sarcastically as she climbed under the covers, "You had to go to Florida. See what you get. How can you prove you didn't kill him?"

"I'm thinking," said Jay in a way he was guilty. "If the police come by, I got some explaining to do."

******

First thing Thursday morning, the investigator entered the Golf Shop. He handed the clerk a tape and said, "We made photos of all your visitors." He spread the photos on the counter. "Which one you recognize as the man you've seen before?"

The clerk viewed twenty photos of each customer who played yesterday. He shook his head and said, "This customer got a cart after Mr. King, but according to the register, he finished all eighteen holes."

The investigator said, "Did Mr. King finish before him?"

"No," said the clerk. "I left after the customer left the shop. Now Mr. King could have let him go ahead of him. These are the photos that came in after that customer, and I know all of them, but I don't think they knew Mr. King."

The investigator asked, "Did anything out of the ordinary happen?"

"Yes sir," said the clerk. "Mr. King mentioned something about a shareholders meeting."

The investigator said, "Thanks for your cooperation." He turned and left.

The investigator and a detective got into the car. They drove off.

The investigator said, "Let's go to the airport and breeze through some airlines manifests. It's the only thing we got to go on." He verged onto I-95.

******

Frank felt guilty that morning. He was too tired to make it to Palmer's. He rolled in his bed, picked up the phone, and dialed Cookie. Her phone rang, but there was no answer. He hung up and went back to sleep.

*****

Cookie's house phone rang, but she didn't answer. She was trying to get enough rest to make it through the day. Cookie's desire was to be fresh for tomorrow.

Cookie was nude on her bed. The floral quilt was at the foot of the bed and most of the top sheet had slouched to the floor. She went to the bathroom, put down the toilet seat, and used it. After she washed her hands, she respected the washcloth germs at the sink and dropped it into the hamper. She went back into the bedroom, threw on an oversized NY tee, and then went to the kitchen to fix something to eat.

*****

Crook woke up. He rolled out of bed and went to the bathroom. After he brushed his teeth, he got into the shower. He decided there was no need to shave his whiskers. Besides, he'll get a haircut and shave tomorrow before the show.

Crook couldn't decide on whether to wear a suit or dress in a sport coat and trousers. What the hell, he was only going to his shop. After he got dressed, he headed for Crook's Outlet.

*****

Sam Lovely waited at the Alton Arena. All the models were accounted for except one, Cookie. Everything was built around the catwalk. Sam figured if they practice before the stage crew arrive, it would be profitable.

Before long, Cookie entered and said, "Sorry I'm late."

Sam said, "Yes, you're sorry and you're late." He looked at all the models and said, "Girls and boys, let's practice your walk."

The women and men models walked down the runway. When they got to the end, they turned around and walked up. They did the walk twice.

Sam said, "Now let's walk with the first set in mind. The bedroom attire."

The models began to walk.

Sam said, "Remember the theme is the sea. Wiggle a little babies."

The models did as instructed and stopped when they had arrived back at the beginning.

Sam said, "Next, let's practice the athletic and exercise set."

The models did as ordered and returned to the beginning.

Sam said, "Now let's practice the casual. Remember the theme is the sea. Pretend you are headed for the beach." He clapped and said, "Let's go ladies."

The models did as ordered, but Cookie stumbled. When they got back to the beginning, they snickered.

Sam said, "What the hell was that? Girls and boys, we have to be perfect. The audience is not forgiving. We're going to do it again. This time do it right."

The models marched down the catwalk and returned without incident.

Sam clapped and said, "Bravo, bravo. Now, let's work on the evening attire."

The models completed the set.

Sam said, "Now girls and boys, let's practice the pivot…

******

Jitterbug sat at a table in Maggie's Café. A waitress brought over bacon, eggs, grits with toast, and a tiny glass of orange juice. Keith and Gin German walked in and sat at his table.

Jitterbug shoveled grits and eggs into his mouth. He looked up and said, "If you hungry, let me know."

Keith said, "We've already ate, but go ahead and enjoy your meal."

Jitterbug took a bite of toast and said as he chewed, "Yes, I beat the crap out of Baby Ray."

Keith said, "Thanks."

"What?"

Keith said, "That was my job." He reached into his pocket and handed Jitterbug three $100 dollar bills. "That's your share."

"Well, looka here," said Jitterbug as he sat back.

Keith said, "I'm a fair man. I know you're planning something with Jay. Maybe we can convince him to let us in on it."

"Too late," said Jitterbug. "The show is tomorrow. What I can do is convince him to let you in on the next deal."

Keith sat back, looked around, and said, "Cool. Meet us at Alton's Nest and we'll discuss it."

Jitterbug stuck the last slice of bacon in his mouth and said, "Sounds good. I'll be there at the usual time."

******

Marge and Cheryl traveled up 15th Street in Marge's Land Rover Defender. Apartments, roadhouse, and businesses flashed by. Steely Dan played on the radio.

Marge said, "Remember to make sure there're no loose strings. All the costumes are ready. We're Haute couture so all we have to do is double check each garment." She paused, turned into the parking garage, and said, "Adjust Niger's costumes to fit Eddie."

"Anything else?" said Cheryl.

Marge said, "Call Janice and make sure she meet us at Alton Arena after lunch. Also call Warren to remind him the models will be coming today as soon as they finish practice."

Cheryl said, "The limo service called to make sure everything was a go. I called Reese's Deep Sea to make sure they knew everything was a go."

Marge parked in her slot at Angels Incorporated and they got out. They strolled into the sewing room where there were racks of clothes that lined the walls. There were a station for each set. In each set were two sections; one for ladies and the other for men.

Sowing machines whined, scissors snipped, and yards of cloth had been cut. Marge walked in a sweatshirt and sweatpants with Nikes among them to make sure everything was proper. Cheryl went to each set to make sure there were some adjustments to Niger's costume to fit Eddie's measurements. His measurements were; 40-32-34 with size eleven footwear.

******

The demolition experts arrived at the Alton Arena. They unloaded several boxes of small explosives. An armed guard in casual clothes was posted at the door. Once inside, they went to work. Miniature explosives were placed around the catwalk. A man walked up to the guard at the door.

The guard said, "Identification please."

Frank Ross pulled out his pass and handed it to the guard.

The guard examined it and said, "Okay."

Frank walked in and said, "Didn't know you worked this early in the morning."

A burley supervisor walked over to him with a half-smile painted on his face and asked, "Who are you?"

Frank noticed all workers had a pistol strapped to their waist or in a shoulder harness. He said, "Frank Ross, your advisor."

The supervisor scratched his head and said, "Have you ever worked with munitions?"

"No," said Frank. "But I was hired by Marge Gray."

The supervisor said, "Well, that's between you and her. I don't collaborate with people I don't know." He patted his holstered pistol. "We got work to do. The door is right there and if you don't leave, I'll have to shoot ya."

Frank threw up his hands, backed from the supervisor, turned, and left.

******

While the special effects team worked, DJ Hoss approached the guard.

The guard said, "Identification please."

Hoss gave him their passes and said, "We're here to setup our equipment."

"Okay, go ahead."

Hoss went in with his assistant. They placed some of their equipment in the proper area and began to wire it.

******

Penny had left Jay's apartment just before nine. She had to make sure the fashions were within their standards. Jay stayed home. He wasn't pressed for anything. There was a knock at his door. Jay opened it and there stood Crook.

Crook said, "Wake up. Let's go get some breakfast."

"Breakfast," said Jay, "you wake me for breakfast?"

Crook said, "Don't have a choice. I'm hungry as a dog."

"All right. Let me put some clothes on." Jay walked to his bedroom.

Crook looked around and said, "Do you get tired of slumming?"

Jay said from the bedroom, "No, it gives me a break from people kissing my butt."

Crook said, "Let's go to Maggie's. Her breakfast are slamming."

Jay hollered from his bedroom, "Haven't had a home cooked meal in years." He walked from his bedroom dressed. He grabbed his car keys and said, "Let's go."

They parked on the side of Maggie's. When they entered the café, a waitress said, "Let me seat you." She turned and they followed her. She placed the menus on the table and left.

"I'll be ready by six," said Crook.

Jay said, "That'll be good to know. Who do you think is the fake?"

The waitress returned and stood at their table.

Jay looked to her and said, "The regular breakfast with cream and sugar, please."

Crook said, "I'll have the same with coffee, black."

Jay said, "Why did you stop by?"

"Wanted to ask you, where is the after party?"

Jay said, "At the arena. Invited guest are the only ones allowed."

"I've got to meet with some guys later on at Alton's Nest after the show."

Jay said, "You can do whatever you want after the show, but now you have to understand you have to be cautious. Mickey is dead."

"I'll be careful," said Crook. "But my friends want to know will you turn them on to your next deal?"

Jay said, "I'll have to think about that. I'm not a bank."

The waitress brought their breakfast to the table. She placed the plates and juice in front of them. She then poured coffee in two porcelain cups and placed condiments on the table.

Chapter 9

Guess Who Killed Mickey?

By now it was mid-morning. The investigator saw a name on a manifest, Julius Wilbur. He associated the name with the shareholder's meeting, and then he called the FBI office in Flight 106 destination.

Investigator Mel said, "I've got some information on a murder, but it's out of my jurisdiction. Can you check it out?"

Agent Stanford said, "Sure, we can give you a hand. What's his name and address."

"Name, Julius Wilbur," said Mel. "Address, apartment three-o-six in The Leisure."

Agent Stanford said, "Got it all down. Anything else?"

"Can I come and observe?"

Agent Stanford said, "Of course, we want the right perpetrator. When are you coming?"

"I'll be there this afternoon and will leave Saturday morning."

Agent Stanford said, "Great, can't wait to see you." He hung up.

******

Barry Crook Johnson story goes like this. His father was the former drummer for a jazz band called The Notes. His mother worked for a baker on Washington Avenue. He was brought up in Harlem Projects, which was where working families lived. In spite of the fact, it was a rough neighborhood. It would have helped some police to live there since that's where they spent most of their time. As a teenager, he played real cops and robbers. On many occasions he was arrested for burglary and shoplifting. Bartolome Johnson was an undisputable truant.

When he turned eighteen, his life changed. He met a thug named Gin Gordon. Well one day, Gin Gordon was in a fight with another teen. The other kid was beating the crap out of Gin Gordon. Bartolome jumped in to help, but he too got beat down. Neither of them expected what was to happen; they started to receive respect from the Carinii crime syndicate.

It turned out, Gin Gordon's father was a hoodlum. Bartolome and Gin wanted to make a lot of cash. So, the Carinii member assigned them to an easy job; to collect from businesses that were being extorted. However, before too long they got busted.

They were convicted and did a six month stretch in Rikers. There, they maneuvered their way into narcotics. This is what happened.

Convicted Sonny Carinii was doing a stretch for stolen credit cards. However, he was the main heroin dealer for the Carinii organization. Sonny needed someone who could hold their own.

The convicts were in the prison compound. Muscular convicts grunted as they lifted weights, some of them huffed as they played basketball while others walked the compound. Sonny, Bartolome, and Gin Gordon strolled the yard. All convicts were under the careful eyes of armed correction officers on ramps above the compound.

Sonny said to Bartolome and Gin, "Keep ya mouth shut. Don't tell 'em nothing. When ya'll get out, I'll have something for ya."

Gin Gordon asked, "Whatcha got for us? We ain't snitches."

"You'll see what I got my man," said Sonny.

Bartolome said, "For now on call me Barry. Don't want to be lame."

Sonny said with laughter, "Barry? How about Crook? You're a hard man. You'll wear that name well. As for you." He pointed at Gin. "Your attitude is like a German; ya wanna run everything. You'll be called Gin German."

When Crook and Gin German got out, they were set up in the drug trade. That's where they made their fortune.

One day two hustlers disappeared. They had gotten ripped off by a rival dealer. Carinii's men were hunted down and killed. Crook was sick of looking over his shoulder. So, he convinced the Carinii organization to open Crook's Clothing Outlet. They agreed as long as he remained connected to them. Which meant, as long as they got a piece of the action, and their slices were unfairly large, but he agreed.

Crook wiped his hands with a napkin, stood, and said to Jay, "Catch you this afternoon at Alton's."

"Sure," said Jay. He rose from the table, and they left.

******

Gin German was no stranger to the streets. Most of the people in the neighborhood respected him. His charisma was huge; his heart was cold.

Once he broke a man's girlfriend arm because the man dodged him. He wanted to send a message; no one can hide. Gin German went to Ray's Corner Mart to buy some cigarettes. While he was at the counter, a Carinii walked in.

Sonny Carinii said, "Hey, parmesan Gin German."

"What's up?," said Gin German.

"When did you get in the free?"

Sonny said, "I've been out for about a year." Someone caught his attention.

A blond lady was heading to the counter.

Sonny said, "That's the guy's girlfriend."

Gin German spun around and spotted her. He pointed and asked, "Her? Are ya sure?"

"That's her."

Gin German waited until she stood behind Sonny. He said to her, "You can come and get in front of me."

"Sure, that's nice of you," she said with a smile."

As soon as she stood in front of him, a fat hand slapped across her mouth, and an arm put her in a half nelson. The clerk looked on in fear when he heard a pop. Tears streamed from her eyes as she struggled.

Gin German said, "Tell that punk." He lifted her off the floor and continued, "To pay up by tonight or I'll break the other arm." He let her go and left.

Sonny walked to the counter and bought a cigar. As for the lady, she went to the hospital. Doctors patched her up and called the police. When the police arrived, they had questions. They had questions she couldn't answer. The reason was simple; there weren't any snitches in that neighborhood.

That story was told for one reason. Gin German was a man no one should tangle with. Jay Wilbur was in his cross hairs.

******

Models began to arrive at Clippers.

Warren ushered them, "Ladies and gentlemen, come on in." He would point to a vacant chair and went on, "Take that chair and we'll be right with you."

Penny walked in and went straight to Warren.

Warren said to Pat Needles, "Take care of the arrivals and seat them. Ladies on this side and boys on the other side."

Pat nodded.

Warren said, "What do you need?"

"I have this last minute replacement that require a different cut."

Warren said, "Which one?"

She pointed at Eddie Grant and said, "That one."

Warren gasped and whispered, "That one? He's gorgeous. I'll fix him up nicely."

He handed Penny a chart and said, "Which cut?"

She searched through the styles and tapped, "That one."

"Are you sure? I have a fresh style that's not on the chart. Let me show you." He walked to a desk, opened a drawer, and returned to her. He said, "This is the one. Guarantee no man around here have this cut."

Penny was stunned. She purred, "Wow." She examined the cut and said to Eddie, "Come here."

Eddie walked over and said, "You need me?"

"Yes I do. Take that chair and get this cut."

Eddie looked at the cut and said, "You ain't got to tell me twice." He went and got in Warren's barber chair.

Leola entered and went straight to Penny. She said, "How long will this take? I've got a commercial to do around twelve."

Penny said to Warren, "Bump Cira to this afternoon and take Leola now."

Warren went over to Cira and whispered, "You been change to two o'clock this afternoon."

Cira nodded, got out of the chair, and stormed out while Penny yelled, "Cira, Cira!"

Cira brushed Cookie as she stormed out. Cookie walked in and sat in a chair to wait until any barber's chair was empty. She picked up a magazine and began to thumb through it.

******

At Alton Arena, Marge and Cheryl walked passed the armed guard into the arena. Hammers pounded, plywood walls were erected, and music blasted from two gigantic JBLs. The catwalk was complete. The special effects supervisor came from backstage and approached them.

The supervisor said, "We are all done here. I'll be here early tomorrow afternoon. Ed," he pointed at the armed guard, "and two other security guards will take shifts throughout the night."

Marge said, "Splendid."

The supervisor said, "A guy came by claiming you hired him to recommend us. I told him I don't work with anyone I don't know. Had to chase him off."

"Thanks. There was a misunderstanding," said Marge as she continued, "He was supposed to aid you if you needed him. He'll be backstage with one of the models."

The supervisor said, "He haven't even worked with munitions. Just keep him away from us. Like I told him, stay away from the stage or I'll have to shoot him." He walked to the guard.

Marge and Cheryl walked to the sound booth. The music stopped abruptly. DJ Hoss showed plumbers crack when he kneeled behind the turntables stand. He stood and turned to the control console. One of his ears was covered with one of the earphones. His other hand scratched records.

Hoss looked up and saw Marge and Cheryl as they stood in front of the booth. He set the earphones down, cut the music off, and said, "What can I do for you?"

Marge said, "Nothing. Sounds like you got everything under control."

Cheryl added as she looked around, "Cee Note is going to be blown away."

"Don't know about all that," said Hoss, "he's a big dawg. But I know how to keep 'em pleased."

Marge and Cheryl turned to face the catwalk and the walls. Labors were as ants when they hoisted a lighthouse in the middle of the stage at the end of the catwalk.

Sonny Carinii approached Marge and Cheryl after they got into Marge's Land Rover. He said, "A dear friend of my organization was killed. I'm looking for Julius Wilbur."

Marge looked out of her window and said, "He's not around. Sorry about your friend, but I gotta go." She backed out of her slot and drove off.

Marge said, "Julius Wilbur organization helped finance the show. I'm going to call Penny and tell her. That goon wants more than a chit-chat."

*****

Agent Stanford walked into Angels Inc.

A tailor stepped to him and said, "May I help you?"

"I'm Agent Stanford of the FBI." He flashed his badge. "I'm looking for Marge Gray. Is she in?"

"No, she went to the arena."

"Tell her, I'm looking for Julius Wilbur." He handed the tailor a business card and continued, "It will be of great help if she can give me his where about." He turned and left.

*****

Cookie grabbed a Whooper for lunch at Burger King. Pat Russell put his foot in her hair style. She had covered her hair with a scarf to keep it fresh. When she turned to leave, Agent Stanford stepped into her path.

Stanford said, "I'm Agent Stanford." He flashed his badge and went on, "Heard you may know where Julius Wilbur worked, hung out, and lived."

"Sorry pal," said Cookie, "Don't know what you're talking about." She tried to sidestep him, but he stepped into her path.

Stanford said, "If I find out you're lying, I'll run you in for obstruction of justice. He's a person of interest in a murder. Now, can you tell me where he live?"

"No but he'll be at the fashion show tomorrow. You know, the one at Alton Arena."

Jitterbug walked out of Maggie's. The two hot dogs he dusted off left him sleepy.

Agent Stanford stepped into his path, flashed his badge, and said, "Do you know Julius Wilbur?"

"Naw man," said Jitterbug.

Stanford said, "We'll he's a person of interest in a murder. If I find out you're lying, you will be prosecuted to the full length of the law."

"Like I said, I don't know him, but I can tell you who do," said Jitterbug, "Checkout this cat called Crook."

Stanford asked holding a pen and pad, "What's his name and where does he live?"

"His name is Barry Johnson, and he lives…"

******

Crook walked to answer his apartment door.

When he opened it, Agent Stanford said, "I'm trying to find out where Julius Wilbur live. Heard you know. Now if you lie to me, Bartolome Johnson, I'll prosecute you."

"Why are you coming at me so strong?"

Stanford said, "He's a person of interest in a murder."

Crook knew Stanford was on to his hustle. If he lied, he'll be convicted. He had no choice but to tell what he knew. Crook said, "I supposed to meet him tonight at Alton's Nest."

Stanford said, "Thanks for your cooperation." He turned and left.

******

Agent Stanford called Investigator Mel and said, "Be ready to hit the ground running tonight. I have a lead tonight and a lead tomorrow."

Mel responded, "I'm ready. As soon as my flight land, pick me up."

******

Jay phone rang in his apartment. He answered, "Yeah?"

Penny said, "Marge told me to tell you a goon is looking for you."

"Why and what's his name?"

Penny said, "He claimed a friend of his organization was lost and he's looking for you. Marge said he didn't look like he wanted to talk."

"What does he look like," asked Jay.

Penny said, "Marge described him as white, thick, and a match for you."

"Okay, thanks," said Jay and he hung up.

There's a knock at the door. Jay answered.

When he opened the door, Crook walked into the apartment and said, "Agent Stanford is looking for you. The FBI is in the case now. He called you a person of interest for a murder. It's probably Mickey's murder."

"This is strange," said Jay, "Penny called and said a stout White guy was looking for me. Now you're saying the FBI is looking for me." Jay thought and calmly said, "What did you tell 'em?"

Crook said, "I told him where you lived. Jitterbug told me the agent questioned him. He told the agent to see me. Now I'm seeing you. I told 'em I'm supposed to meet you tonight at Alton's. Sorry brother."

"You didn't do anything wrong," said Jay, "I'll control it."

******

Cookie banged on Frank's apartment door.

Frank opened the door and asked, "What's wrong?"

"The FBI stopped me and ask about Jay. He said Jay is a person of interest."

Frank said, "Jay claimed he was down there for a meeting. It's funny how he flew back, and his partner is dead. Maybe he did kill him."

"All the money he has," said Cookie, "Why would he do that?"

"To get more money by keeping Mickey's share," said Frank, "That's the way rich guys think. I always figured he was a fake. He's gonna get what's coming. All I have to do is trap 'em."

Chapter 10

Watch Your Back Someone's Watching

Keith and Gin German knocked on Jitterbug's apartment door.

Jitterbug opened it and said, "What ya'll want?"

Keith said, "Can we come in?"

Jitterbug stepped aside. Keith and Gin German walked in.

Keith said, "Heard you were taking to the FBI." It was a lie. Keith saw him when he left Maggie's.

"No," said Jitterbug, "he asked me about Julius Wilbur."

Keith said, "What did they ask?"

"Questions like where he lived," Jitterbug said while he waved his hand, "which I don't know. So, I gave him Crooks address. The agent claimed Julius Wilbur was a murder suspect."

Keith shook his head and said, "If we only did business right." That fortified his reason to pick up surveillance of Jay.

Gin German asked, "What now?"

Keith said, "We can take care of Crook and Jay will get the blame. We have got to do it tonight. The show is tomorrow, and Jay may be arrested or skip town. Jitterbug, you'll have to do it. They won't suspect you."

"Everybody knows I can get close to Crook because I'm Crook's partner," Jitterbug said as he walked to the window, "But if ya'll take care of Crook, Jay will be suspect. He and Crook have something going on. It would look like a double cross."

Keith said, "That sounds like a plan. I knew I was right."

They laughed.

Gin German said, "Ya know that will make Sonny Carinii angry and he will want revenge. So, we got to be careful."

"That's even better," said Keith, "Sonny Carinii and the FBI will be after Jay. It depends on who will get to him first. Sonny will order a hit and the FBI will order his arrest."

Jay changed into a white tux with black bowtie, coma bond, and pants at Nordstrom. He stood in front of a mirror and noticed Frank standing behind him. He turned and said, "Didn't know you needed a tux too."

Frank walked up to him and said, "That looks good on ya. But I rather wear a black tux jacket. Can I ask ya something?"

"Sure."

Frank said, "The FBI told Cookie you're a suspect in a murder. I think you're a fake. Did ya do it?"

"What if I did," said Jay, "It's none of your business."

Frank didn't want to press the issue because if he did, Frank may end up missing. He said, "Forget about it. You're not a killer."

Jay turned to face the mirror and said, "Now you're beginning to know me."

Frank was relieved, but he still believed Jay had killed someone. If he were innocent, the FBI wouldn't be on his trail.

******

Marge answered her phone, "Angels Inc."

"This is Roy Clark. How you're doing?"

Marge said, "Great how can I help you?"

"You can start by commenting on this rumor," said Roy. "Heard Julius Wilbur might be in a shake down."

Marge said, "Naw, a goon was looking for him. Where did you hear that?"

"Heard it from Penny," said Roy, "Also heard he was a suspect in a murder."

Marge said, "Now you see how wild it's getting. He couldn't harm anyone."

"Well," said Roy, "he's an ex-boxer and money is involved. How do you know he doesn't want to cut out his partners? All I'm say is, we want our profits from the show."

Marge said, "You'll get your profit. Why do you worry over rumors?"

"Because it's my banks money," said Roy, "And if I lose one penny, I can go to jail. Want to join me?"

Marge remained silent.

"Good," said Roy, "Break a leg." He hung up.

Cheryl walked into the office.

Marge said, "Have Julius Wilbur come and see me."

******

Crook and Jitterbug went into a bar off Benjamin Avenue. The low light with hanging plants soothe the soul. *Sweet Caroline* played over the intercom. A coy, plump bartender leaned against the liquor shelves reading a newspaper.

Crook and Jitterbug sat at the bar. The bartender bounced off the shelves and said to Crook and Jitterbug, "What do you want to drink."

Crook said, "Rum and coke."

Jitterbug said, "Tom Collins."

He started to work on the drinks.

Crook said, "Can't wrap my mind around Jay being a murderer."

Jitterbug said, "In my business, I meet all kinds of characters. I knew this guy who would borrow money from people. When it came time to pay it back, he'll kill them just to keep from paying them off." Jitterbug paused before he continued, "I know this other guy who would set up a deal, bring you in on it, and then kill ya after he received the money."

Crook took it all in. The last example fitted Jay's motive operandi. Bring him in on the deal, and then kill him when he gets the money. Crook said, "Thanks, you can never be too careful."

The bartender placed their drinks in front of them.

******

Alberto's Design was a jewelry store on 18th Street. The jewelry sold in the store was custom made. Alberto Oppenheimer was Alberto's Design jeweler. His client list was longer than a who's who directory.

Alberto had completed the finish touches when one of his most loyal customers entered the store. Janice Merlin strolled to the counter.

Janice said, "Darling, you called and said the bracelets and jewelry were ready." She looked at the work of art jewelry in the glass displays."

Alberto said, "You are correct. Let me get the items you asked for." He pulled the jewelers' examination glass from his eye and went to the back room.

He returned with seven small boxes and an armed security guard. Alberto said, "These are the items you requested and here is the sponsorship." He handed her a stuffed yellow envelope and laid all of the valued pieces on the counter.

She said, "There's no need to check each box because I know you do excellent work. I'll check this one." She opened a small box and gasped. The white gold, feminine wrist bracelet had a pearl on each side of the name plate. It was an uncomplicated design, but the size of the pearls used to create it was unflawed.

Alberto watched as she examined the valued item.

She proclaimed, "It's beautiful. I know exactly who's going to wear it."

Alberto placed the jewelry in a satchel and said, "Thanks for your business. By the way, how's Marge?"

"She's great," said Janice, "She's got a new lover." She smiled, turned, and walked to the door.

Just as she walked out of the door, Cee Note, Buddy Webb, Sharky, and Antony Howell was approaching it.

She greeted Cee Note, "Morning darling," and continued out of the door.

Cee Note went into the shop with his entourage behind him. He said cheerfully, "Ah kardaş, nasilinez."

"Ah Cee Note," said Alberto, "No work today?" He walked up to Cee Note and kissed him on both cheeks. "Wait until you see it." He went to the back.

Antony, Sharky, and Buddy Webb browsed the display cases.

Tall Buddy Webb in Knicks practice and sweats said to Cee Note, "He got some dope stuff."

"The last time I was here," said Sharky with several gold necklaces, "His rings were straight."

Antony in a Scot plaid sportscoat said with a mellow voice, "Can't believe he makes all this stuff."

"Well, he does," said Cee Note.

Alberto return from the back room. He said with enthusiasm, "Look at this."

Cee Note held a woman diamond engagement ring. It had a five karat diamond in the middle with smaller diamonds clustered at the base. The ring was trimmed in eighteen karat gold.

Cee Note said, "WoW."

Alberto handed Cee Note the wedding ring.

Cee Note held it and said, "Too cold. Wrap them up."

Alberto said, "She's going to be overwhelmed when she it. It's my best craftsmanship. There's nothing like it in the world. For you, kardaş, three million dollars."

Cee Note handed Alberto an American Express card.

Alberto took the card and began to process it. He said, " when are you going to propose?"

Cee Note said, "Tomorrow night at the finale of the show. She's gonna walk to the end of the catwalk, some special effect will go off, and then she's gonna turn and come to me. I'll cut the music, drop down to one knee, and then bam! I'll propose."

Antony said, "That's cute and all that, but I got a set at Alton's tonight. So, we got to get going."

Alberto gave the wrapped jewelry to Cee Note and said, "Come again."

Cee Note nodded, turned from Alberto, and they left the store.

******

Jay went into Angel Inc. office.

Cathy said, "Marge is waiting for you. She picked up the phone and said, "He's here."

Jay heard Marge through the receiver, "Send him in."

Jay said as he closed in, "Heard you wanted to see me."

"I did," said Marge, "I need to know one thing; when the show is over will I have to look for money?"

Jay sat and said, "Why would you do that?"

"Roy Clark called and told me something interesting."

"Before I tell you," said Marge, "Why was that goon looking for you?"

Jay said, "A lot of men are looking for me. It's nothing big."

"It is if I was told you murdered someone. Roy Clark is hanging that over this show and threaten to pull out if this is true."

Jay had to think fast. He said, "If I did it, it would be for a good reason, profit. But that's my business. It has nothing to do with your show."

"That's all I wanted to hear," Marge said and continued, "I'll be relieved when this show is over. Then maybe I can get a breather."

Jay stood and said, "See you tomorrow night." He turned and left her office.

******

Leola and another model Nicki were in Nordstrom women clothing department. She said to the clerk, "Here to pick up my blouse, jeans, and shoes."

The clerk said, "Sure." She turned and left the floor.

Nicki said, "What's it like?"

"What do you mean?"

Nicki said, "What's it like to date Cee Note? It's a dream come true for any girl."

"Dreamy," said Leola, "I've never met anyone like him. He isn't overbearing and he trust me too much. I could date a lot of men, but I don't. I love him."

"Does he loves you?"

Leola said, "Those kind of men will treat you right, but that doesn't mean they love you. He's on the road all the time. So, he's probably humping girls in different cities."

"Why don't you let some other man stroke you. You're gone all the time too."

Leola said, "I'm gonna let you in on a secret. I got a crush on Jay Dub. That man does it for me. Penny try to be all proper, but she doesn't know I'm gonna hook up with him tomorrow night after the after party."

"From what I heard, Jay maybe in jail."

Leola said, "I heard the same thang too. I even heard he killed somebody, and the FBI is looking for him. That really turned me on."

"That's nothing new," said Nicki, "You always date guys accused of murder."

Leola said, "Cee Note was accused and acquitted of murder. Jay is authentic. That's why we're gonna take my private jet out of the country tomorrow night after the party. It's all setup. We're gonna fly to Belize."

"You shouldn't get mixed up in all that drama. Who knows, he may kill you."

The clerk returned with the clothes and said, "You wanna try them on?"

"That's okay," said Leola to the clerk, "Just package them up."

******

Jitterbug and Gin German went into Perry's Hallway, a bar on the lower eastside. They sat at a table and munched on peanuts.

Jitterbug said, "Can't wrap my mind around Jay a murderer. Why would he do that? He's loaded."

Gin German reasoned, "He maybe an imposter; you know a fake."

"Man, he fooled us. What I don't get is why do Keith want Crook dead."

Gin German said, "Keith knows if Jay killed someone, Sonny Carinii will come looking for him. If Crook is alive, he can protect Jay. But if he's gone, Sonny Carinii can get to Jay."

"So, Keith claimed it had to be tonight," said Jitterbug.

Gin German said, "And get this, I'm supposed to do the job."

"How you're gonna do it?"

Gin German said, "Don't know, but I'll need a distraction to carry it out."

A waitress came to them and said, "What will you have?"

Jitterbug ordered, "Malibu and orange."

Gin German ordered, "Jameson Irish whisky neat."

She turned and went to the bar.

Jitterbug said to Gin German, "Have ya done your homework?"

"Heard he's gonna be at Alton's tonight to catch Antony Howell's show. If I can get someone to start a distraction when Crook leave, I can follow him outside and take care of it."

Jitterbug said, "Thought you and Crook were tight. Ya'll spent a stretch together, delt drugs, and were associates of Sonny Carinii."

"That doesn't mean squat," said Gin German, "If Sonny Carinii gives you a job, you take it."

A waitress brought their drinks to the table. Jitterbug paid her and said, "Thanks."

Gin German said, "It would be a significant help if you would do the job. I'll never forget it."

"No thanks," said Jitterbug, "I use my fist to hurt people, but I'm not a killer. Why don't you ask Jay to do it? He's accused of murder."

Gin German said, "You may be on to something."

******

Jay walked into his apartment. He cut on his television and sat on the couch. The Dramatics *Whatcha See is Whatcha Get* video appeared on MTV. There was a knock at the door. Jay got up, looked through the peep hole, and opened the door.

Penny walked in and said, "Marge told me you may have killed someone. Is that true?"

Jay said, "Have a seat."

She sat. Jay went on, "Do you think I could kill someone?"

"Don't know I'm confused," Penny said and continued, "Why would you want to be with me when you're one step away from prison? I'll tell you why. You're a son of a bitch. You bastard."

Jay said coolly, "Well, it shouldn't matter now. If that's what you think," Jay pointed, "There's the door."

Raydio's *You Can't Change That*, played over his audio system.

She stood, walked defiantly to the door, turned, and said with tears, "Can't you see I'm in love with you?" She walked out of the door.

Raydio sang, "You're the one I love, and you can't change that."

Jay closed the door, but before he could sit on his couch, someone knocked. He opened the door and there stood Leola.

Leola said, "Can I come in?"

"Sure," said Jay.

She stepped in, looked around and said, "Why do you live in this dump? Are you slumming?"

"No, can I help you?"

Leola said, "The other day when we were talking, I wasn't kidding about going to Belize. And I was thinking would you want to go?"

"I thought about your offer, but I noticed Cee Note is sweet on you."

Leola said, "I can oversee him. But you need to get out of this country; murderer."

"Christ, everybody knows," said Jay, "Why you want me to go with you?"

Leola said, "You're a big boy. Use your imagination." She uncrossed her legs and sat seductively.

"Look, your offer sounds great, but I don't want anyone to know our plan. I don't want you to get involved."

She stood, kissed him on his cheek, and said, "After the party. I'll be waiting in my Lear jet."

Jay said, "Sure. We can make that happen."

She covered her head with a scarf and her eyes with sunglasses and left.

Jay's phone rang. He answered, "What you got?"

Crook said, "Heard you're a murderer. I was told to watch my back when I'm with you. Want to know did you do it?"

"If I did, it won't change things by tomorrow night. You hang around murderers all the time and you're still here. Don't worry, my situation doesn't conflict with yours."

Crook said, "Going to Antony Howell's show at Alton's tonight. Wanna join me?"

Jay paused and said, "I can't. Don't want to get arrested in a club. I'll see you tomorrow night at the show."

"If you say so," said Crook, "Watch your back, these cats know you're a killer. I'm surprised no one has given you up."

"I'm off the streets until tomorrow night," said Jay, "I can't go to Alton's. Can't afford to take that chance."

Crook said, "I understand. But if you ask me for my advice, I'll tell you to take the first thing smoking outta here. Heard FBI agents are all around here."

"If I get a chance," Jay said, "I will leave after the after-party tomorrow."

Crook said, "Where you're going?"

"Don't know," said Jay, "Maybe I'll take Leola up on her offer and go to Belize."

Crook said, "Be cool," and hung up.

Jay knew something was up. Crook was trying to protect him from Sonny Carinii. Sonny Carinii actions would be an act of vengeance for Mickey. Keith and Gin German wanted him out of the way so they could get to Crook. Crook was an influential man in the syndicate. If he were killed, they could take over his businesses. Frank Ross is willing to turn him in for a reward and that way no one would know he was broke. Jitterbug wanted no part of the deal. The FBI was out to arrest him, but all Marge cared about was that fashion show. Out of all those worries, Jay's biggest worry was the FBI. They always get their man.

Chapter 11

Love Hurts in a Good Way

Eddie Grant jogged in a good mood. He sprinted in the park with a feeling like the rest of the world, content. Bitterness had abandon his heart. In fact, he felt like he was beginning to love again.

Yesterday while he was sweeping the floor, Leola and her entourage walked in. He did a double take and stared. She was stunningly beautiful. She walked passed him without a thought.

He said aloud, "Miss Leola, You're so good-looking."

Leola turned and said, "You too." She turned, went to the dressing room, and sat in Pat's chair.

"You too," stuck in Eddie's mind. He believed if he could land stardom, he could have her. He followed her and when she sat in a saloon chair, he stepped to her and said, "Mice roam silently at night."

Leola looked at him, chuckled, and said, "Is that the best you can do? Honey, you need a coach." She settled in her chair.

Pat lectured Leola as he picked her hair, "Look at this nappy mess. You should have a barbwire shop."

Eddie went back to sweeping. He was hurt, but in a clever way. Now she knows he exist. That's when he decided to approach her at the after party.

Eddie picked up his jogging speed.

******

Cookie answered her apartment door wearing a halter top and Daisey Dukes. She opened it and Rift, a male model, walked in.

Rift said, "I heard a terrible rumor on the gossip line. I heard one of our producers is a murderer. Have you heard that?"

Cookie said, "The FBI told me. And you know when the FBI is on your trail, most likely you're guilty."

Rift said, "Man, I thought he was an ordinary rich guy. It turned out, he's a killer. What I don't understand is why he's still hanging around?"

"He's trying to tie up loose ends," Cookie said, "Things can't be that loose."

"Girl," said Rift, "You just don't know. He's a killer. All I'm going to do is stay out of his way."

Cookie said, "I don't think he's gonna kill me. I didn't give him up."

"I see," said Rift, "I going to The Farm tonight, wanna go?"

The gay people referred to the White Swallow Nightclub as The Farm. That's where they hung out.

Cookie said, "Thanks, but no thanks. The only thing that place is known for is to pick up gay people and I don't have to worry about anyone looking up my dress."

Rift scolded, "Stuck up heifer. Hope your thing melt together."

Cookie laughed and said as she walked him to the door, "I have a man." She smile and said, "See ya later."

Rift said, "We gone have a blast at the after party. Eddie claimed he's gonna hit on Leola." He laughed."

Cookie said, "Don't see how. I think she's stuck on Cee Note."

******

"Whatta ya mean," Sonny said and continued, "Everybody is looking for this guy. He has to be the one!"

Oriel Carinii, the patriarch of the Carinii organization sat with folded arms. His hair was snow white. His torso was a blimp. His knees hadn't touched in ages. He said, "Don't sound right to me. It sounds like a trap. Let the imposters take care of it, but I want you at the show tomorrow night in case they need our help." Mr. Carinii warned, "But no rough stuff. We'll see him on another day."

******

Inside Harry's Armada on 17th, Cira was dressed in a punk funk outfit. She wore a Jamaican head dress to preserve her hair style for tomorrow. Nicki was dress casual enough to leave little to the imagination. She was with Cira when they browsed the women section for something to augment their outfits for the after party.

Cira said, "Don't know what Leola see in Cee Note."

"The only thing she see is that he's rich," said Nicki.

Cira said, "Money can't get you a love you can feel."

"Oh yes it can," said Nicki, "and much more. You see them with a public eye. I see them as human. When you think about it, Cee Note can't really sing, but his performances rescue him every time."

Cira said, "At first I was captivated. Now, gee whiz Louise, Cee Note is an average dude."

"Now, Eddie Grant is a catch," Nicki said as she felt the fabric of a dress. She continued, "But he's probably a waste."

"Don't think so," said Cira. "I saw him talking to Leola yesterday and it look like she was trying to lead him on."

Nicki said, "Eddie needs to watch himself. Cee Note will kill him if he finds out."

Cira said, "Can't worry about their problems." She placed a dress against her body to size it up and said, "I don't see why they kiss Leola's butt. Yesterday I had to give up my chair for her."

"She's special," Nicki said with laughter.

******

Crook ate at a table in Aswad Orient. An Asian restaurant at the corner of Pine Needles and Covenant Drive on the lower westside. He ordered a porter house steak, a loaded baked potato, and a leafy kelp salad.

Outside, across the street, Keith and Gin German waited in a Caddie.

Keith said, "He's eating early tonight."

"He wants to catch the show," said Gin German as he continued, "Bet he doesn't know it's his last meal."

Keith said, "He doesn't have to know. He should know he's gonna get it."

******

Crook stabbed his steak with his fork, and then forked his potato. It was no surprise, he had to eat dinner alone. All day he noticed people were avoiding him. But it was Jay who got the murder rap.

A server came to his table and asked, "Is everything all right?"

"Perfect," Crook said, "Every hoe has its day."

She frowned and walked away.

He cut his steak and when he stuck the fork in it, he looked up. Janice stood over him.

She said, "How long have you known Jay Dub?"

"About as long as this show," said Crook.

She asked, "Why do you hang with him?"

"Meeting a new friend isn't a crime," he said and continued, "Why are ya'll so up end?"

She said, "Your type had everything under control. What happened?"

"Nothing happened," said Crook, "You need to stick with production. Don't chase ghost that will only bring you down."

******

An American Airline 737 drifted down to the runway. Agent Stanford waited in the terminal at gate six. It wasn't long before the tunnel spewed passengers that increased in numbers. Investigator Mel was among them.

Stanford said, "Investigator Mel?"

"That's me," said Mel, "Tell me what you got."

Stanford said as they walked through the terminal, "I've been questioning people he associates with. I asked for his address to see if they're on the level. I know where he's stays and that's going to be the first place we check."

Mel said, "Do you have photos of anybody that could be an accomplish?"

"Yeah, Barry Crook Johnson," said Stanford, "A local hoodlum associated with Sonny Carinii. But don't worry, he won't bite."

Mel said, "Well, let's rock and roll."

******

Eddie Grant knocked on Cookie's apartment door.

She opened it, smiled, and said, "What the heck you're doing here?"

"Just stopped by to ask you some questions about Leola."

Cookie said cheerfully, "Come in and let's get it done."

He walked in and sat on the couch. She poured a couple of shots, went to the couch, and sat beside him. She handed him a shot glass of liquor and said, "Now what can I do for you?"

"I've got a crush on Leola," Eddie said as he held his drink, "What's she like?"

Cookie said, "A bitch. If you don't pamper her, she won't have anything to do with cha. Cee Note is a fool. She really don't care for him, but he's in a position to build her image. Ya dig."

"How can I get close to her at the after party?"

"Are you serious," said Cookie, "Cee Note will kill you. That's if he don't have someone else do it. My advice is to be careful. I know you want that thang, but it's not worth it if you ask me." She gave him a seductive look and said, "Anything else?"

Eddie caught her hint. She was cute and half naked. He said, "Are you trying to steal Leola's property?"

"I'm a thief so that's all I do," Cookie said as she stood. Her pajama top slid off her shoulders to the floor.

******

Jay woke up from a late afternoon nap. His shirt and shoes was over there beside his leisure chair. His television showed commercials while the air conditioner hummed. There was a knock at the door. He got up to open the door in a tee and chinos. He opened the door and there stood two men. One was tall, impeccably dressed, and appear to be reasonable. The other man was of natural height with some work to do with his appearance.

The tall man said, "I'm Agent Stanford of the FBI." He flashed his badge.

The other man said, "I'm Investigator Mel of Broward County Sheriff Department." He flashed his badge.

Jay looked around outside and said, "Come in."

The men sauntered into the apartment. Agent Stanford looked around with each step. He turned and said, "You're a multimillionaire. Why do you live like this?"

"I live like this to get a break from folks like you."

Stanford said, "I see. Let's cut through the chase. Yesterday you were in Florida, correct?"

"Yes I was, so what?"

Stanford said, "Do you know Mickey King?"

"I do," said Jay.

Stanford said, "Did you know he was murdered yesterday?"

Jay said, "A person on my staff informed me this morning."

"You got all the answers," said Stanford, "So why did you kill him?"

Jay said, "My attorney is William Salter in Palm Beach. I suggest you contact him for any more questions."

"You're a sly little bastard," said Mel.

Jay said, "I'm not sly. I just happen to know my rights. And one of them is; I have the right to remain silent."

Mel said, "Let me tell you one thing. I know you did it. So, either we play these little games, or I'll collect evidence. Either way I'm gonna bust your ass."

"Well then prove it," said Jay, "Now I'm a busy man. So, if you excuse me, I have an appointment.

The men turned and walked to the door. Agent Stanford shook his head.

Investigator Mel said, "Get an air freshener." They left Jay's apartment.

******

Cookie walked passed Stanford and Mel. She went straight to Frank's apartment. She pounded on the door and said, "Frank, it's me."

Frank opened the door, look around outside, and said, "Were you followed?"

She said, "No, why?"

"Those two men down there," he nodded his head, "are staring at you. Come in."

******

Agent Stanford and Investigator Mel descended the stairs.

Stanford said, "It's funny she didn't know where Julius lived, but she knew his neighbor."

Mel said, "She didn't want to be a snitch."

Stanford said, "Let's go get something to eat."
"I'm with ya on that."

******

Antony Howell and sharky vigorously practiced at Raymond's Studio.

The director said, "Let's take five." He left the dance floor.

Antony and Sharky sat in chairs provided by a real estate magnate Winford Richards.

Antony said, "Don't know about you, but I'm ready for tonight's show."

"I'm ready," said Sharky, "But I want it to be right. I wanna be perfect."

"I got to make The Cripple take off," said Antony.

Sharky said, "Ya gotta land your right foot in a smooth motion. If you don't do it that way, you'll really look crippled."

The director said, "Okay fellows, back to work. One two three…"

******

At Lee Cuts right smack in the middle of the ghetto, over on 59th Street, people were scattered on the sidewalk. Children played haphazardly with cars. The gossip corps decorated stoops. Inside Lee Cuts, Crook was in a barber's chair. His haircut was done, therefore he relaxed for a shave."

Jitterbug sat in a lounge chair as he waited his turn. He said to Crook, "Whatcha gonna do tonight?"

"Going to Alton's to catch Antony Howell's show," said Crook.

"That's right," Jitterbug said with excitement, "He's in town for his boy Cee Note's show tomorrow night at the Alton Arena. Cee Note is a chump. He know he killed Piru."

Crook said, "Careful. He was acquitted for that. Nobody knows who killed Piru."

"I bet Baby Ray knows," said Jitterbug with laughter.

A barber yelled, "Next." He looked at Jitterbug.

Chapter 12

Julius Wilbur

Jay sat on his couch. "They know they're gonna get me," he thought.

1997 in Las Vegas at Caesars Palace, the main event was Julius Wilbur vs Austin Reed. Julius was the favored jabber. Reed was the favored body puncher. Both boxers were undefeated. And both boxers were in their prime.

Jay sat on a table while his trainer finished tapping his wrist and hand. Jay said, "What do I need to do to tire him out?"

Mac said as he wrapped Jay's wrist, "Dance mother dance. He can't keep up with ya."

People were sitting elbow to elbow. On the front row were mobsters as well as entertainers. The referee leaned against a neutral corner ropes. The Host and casino delegation were in the center of the ring.

The bass boomed and the drums tapped. Jay shadow boxed his way to the ring. He climbed into the ring and continue to shadow box.

The music changed, and when it did, Reed walked down the aisle to the ring. He climbed into the ring and stood.

The host said, "Now, for our main event, six two and a hundred and twenty three pounds from Harlem, Julius Wilbur!"

The audience cheered as Jay moved to the center throwing punches.

The host said, "His challenger is six four two hundred and twenty four pounds from Phoenix, Austin Reed!"

The audience cheered as Reed moved to the center of the ring pounding his gloves.

The referee checked the boxers gloves as he gave them special instructions.

The referee said, "Gentlemen, come out fighting."

Jay and Reed bumped gloves. They went to their corner. It wasn't long before the bell rang. Both fighters hustled out of their corners.

Jay threw a jab to the face. Reed's head snapped back. Reed threw a pounding punch to Jay's body. Jay folded. When Jay folded, Reed threw a sweeping round house to Jay's left side of his face. Jay staggered back, regrouped, and charged. Reed stood with his guards up. Jay threw an uppercut to Reed's chin and a jab to his face. This battle continued for eleven grueling rounds.

The 12th round was where the match was decided. Reed stood in his corner. Jay remained seated. Reed pointed his gloved fist at Jay's corner. The referee went to Jay's corner and after careful examination, the referee waved his arms. The referee walked to Reed's corner and raised his gloved fist to declare Austin Reed the winner.

In the locker room, Jay was examined, and it was discovered he had a problem with the left side of his face and with his left eye. As a result, he retired from boxing and heavily invested in real estate. That's where he met Mickey King.

******

Keith and Gin German arrived at Alton's early that afternoon. The Notes performed their rendition of Stanley Clark's *Danger Street*. Keith and Gin German sat at a table near the bar.

Keith said, "Heard Crook was going to be here for Antony Howell's show. Therefore, if we're lucky, Jay may show. Either way, Crook has to be gone first. Did you do your homework?"

"Yes, I did," said Gin, "He parks on the Russell side of the club. Few people will be able to see the hit. This job is a piece of cake."

The Note's Nelson Caine, their saxophonist, said while the audience applaud, "Thank you. Thank you very much and thanks for coming out. Our next choice is our rendition of Jerry Cavazos's *Been a long time*. Hit it." He eased into the introduction.

Crook found a parking space on Russell and parked. He walked to the front of Alton's.

Gin German tapped Keith. He pointed at the door as Crook entered the club. Crook eased passed standing customers and made his way to the bar.

He sat and said, "Rum and coke."

The bartender nodded and turned to make his drink.

Crook twist on his stool to watch the band.

Nelson Caine caterwauled as he played the jazz treble notes in the hook. He repeated it over and over until his fuzzed improvised windup faded into the closure of the song.

The audience erupted into a solid applause while The Notes bowed before they left the stage. Alton's intercom music played as the audience settled. And it wasn't long before Antony's backup singers and musicians began to set up the stage.

In the dressing room, Antony said to Cee Note, "Just sit back and relax. I got this. Just want to practice before our Breeze In The Ghetto Tour. You know, work the kinks out."

Cee Note said, "I'm sure you don't need practice. But go ahead bro and do your thang."

They stood, hugged, and Antony left for the stage.

Cee Note entered the audience to find a seat. He was alone. Buddy Webb was in Philadelphia for a game with the 76ers. Sharky had a last minute gig in Vegas at MGM. In looking around, Cee Note spotted an empty stool at the bar.

The stage was set. Jitterbug walked on the stage, grabbed the mike, and said, "Ladies and Gentlemen, you're 'bout to get Horney.

Tonight, The Alton's Nest have Antony Howell to entertain you." He pointed, "Antony Howell."

The audience applauded. A spotlight followed Antony Howell onto the stage. Jitterbug handed him the mike.

Antony sang, "No use to come around cause girl you are Foul." The band played the song with a snazzy beat.

Antony finished *Hate to be Ya* and went into his second song, *Always Together*. It was a slow song with a captive hook; never can I leave you."

Cee Note had to wipe away a tear. It reminded him of his relationship with Leola. He was grateful he was going to propose to her tomorrow night.

Antony finished the song and rushed into a high tempo tune called *Wet Wild*. It was a sexually explicit song and was raw suggested. The audience clapped, stood, and some them rolled their hips.

Crook rose from his stool and made his way to the entrance. Keith and Gin German left their table. When Jitterbug saw Keith and Gin German were leaving, he rushed to the stage.

Antony was winding down when Jitterbug snatched the mike and sang, "Love ain't hot; it's scorching!"

Keith and Gin German stepped outside. They saw Crook walk around the corner. Keith went to his car across the street. Gin German walked to the corner. But before he could turn the corner he heard a pop. It was the sound a pistol. He turned, ran across the street to Keith's Caddie.

Jitterbug stepped outside the club. When he heard the pistol report, he saw Gin German get into Keith's Caddie and it took off. Jitterbug ran to the corner. When he turned the corner, he saw Crook lying beside his car on the sidewalk. His head was in a pool of blood.

People screamed and scattered from the sidewalk. The sirens could be heard at a distance. Jitterbug made his way back into the club. By now the news had hit the inside of Alton's. There was an uneasiness about the atmosphere. As though there was a hush-hush among the patrons.

Frank Ross walked up to Jitterbug and said, "I saw Cee Note and Antony Howell leave in a hurry. What's going on?"

Jitterbug said sorely, "Crook was shot outside."

*****

Agent Stanford and Investigator Mel arrived on scene. Agent Stanford said as they got out of the cruiser and walked to Crook's body, "You can't sit down and eat a meal in this city."

Mel said, "What the hell is happening here?"

Stanford said, "Only one person has assess, opportunity, and capability; Julius Wilbur."

"Let's go check him out," said Mel.

Chapter 12

Fake Alibi

Agent Stanford and Investigator Mel arrive at apartment 306 in The Leisure.

Stanford looked at his watch and said, "It's eleven o'clock pm."

Mel knocked. There was no answer. He knocked harder. There was no answer.

Stanford said, "We'll get him tomorrow night at the fashion show." They left.

******

Penny's phone rang. She answered, "Hello."

"This is Roy. Have you heard?"

"Heard what?"

Roy said, "Crook Johnson was shot near Alton's. Just wanted to make sure you're okay."

"I didn't know that. It's eleven five. When did it happen?"

"About ten minutes ago. Are you okay?"

Penny said, "I'm okay." She hung up.

There was a knock on her door. She looked through the Peep hole and saw Jay. "Someone got shot and he shows up. Bet he's looking for an alibi. Okay, I'll play your silly game," she thought as she opened the door.

Jay said, "Can I come in?"

"It's after eleven and you want to talk to me after what you said to me. Don't think so." She started to close the door, but Jay stuck his foot in the door to block it.

Jay said, "I know you love me, and I love you."

Penny stepped out of the doorway. Jay walked in.

Penny stood with her arms crossed.

Jay said, "Don't put up a defense. I've got somethings going on."

"Bet you do like killing folks," said Penny. "Why do you insist on coming to me?"

"I come to you because I love you."

Penny said, "You know what, after the show, I'll have nothing to do with you. So, if you're not talking about the show," she opened the door, "You can leave."

Jay walked out. She closed the door. She felt he was looking for an alibi. That's why she didn't mention tonight's killing.

******

Cookie knocked on Frank's door. There was no answer. When she turned to leave, the door opened. Frank was a nervous wreck. He was so nervous he was shaking.

"Baby, what's wrong?"

Frank said, "I'm next, baby. I'm next."

Cookie ushered him to the couch. She said, "Don't think that way. Everyone knows Jay's the killer. But we ain't gonna let him get to us. She reached for her purse, opened it, and showed him a pistol.

"Get that thing away from me," said Frank.

She held his jaws and kissed him. She said, "We're gonna be alright."

******

Jay drove passed Alton's and noticed the police car flashing lights. Several police cars blocked off Russell Avenue and wrapped around the curb to the front of Alton's. He drove to a parking space and parked.

As soon as he went into his apartment and closed the door, he heard a knock. He looked through the peep hole before he opened the door.

Jitterbug said as he stepped in, "Have you heard? Crook got shot."

"No, you're the first person to tell me," said Jay.

Jitterbug said, "At first I thought it was Gin German, but I know it wasn't him because I saw him hop into Keith's car and they drove off. Where were you?"

"I have an alibi," said Jay, "I was at Penny's apartment."

Jitterbug didn't buy the alibi. He was convinced Jay shot Crook. Jay must have received the money. He said, "Who would want to kill him?"

"Sonny Carinii," said Jay, "Crook was becoming a liability."

Jitterbug knew Crook was connected with the Carinii and they had no reason to kill him. He decided to go along with Jay's game and said, "Let me check it out. I'll get back with you tomorrow." Jitterbug left with a thought, "Only one man would want Crook dead; the charlatan."

Chapter 13

The Show Must Go On

It was near midnight when Marge woke up to a ringing phone. Groggy she answered, "Yeah."

Penny said, "Jay did it. He killed Barry Johnson at Alton's Nest."

"How do you know that?"

Penny said, "Roy called me when it happened. Not even five minutes later, Jay shows up. I know he was looking for an alibi."

"What did he say?"

Penny said, "Talking about how he loves me. I told him after the show, I won't have anything to do with him."

"Are you going to bring him to the show?"

Penny said, "I'll do that. But after that, we're finished." Penny hung up, but she couldn't shake the feeling; she loved him. It's going to be hard, but she has to move on.

Marge hung up. She had come to the realization that it was a lost cause, but she wasn't going to allow it to affect the show. The show must go on. She cuddled under the sheets and went back to sleep.

******

Agent William Stanford of the FBI was a security specialist in the United States Air Force. His career started when he was assigned to the 48th Tactical Squadron at RAF Lakenheath in the United Kingdom.

One night, Airman Stanford was posted in the weapons storage area. He had finished his meal in a watch tower post when he noticed a vehicle lights pause across from the weapon storage area on the taxiway. The lights of the vehicle stayed on. After a brief time, a shadow appeared to be approaching the fence perimeter.

Airman Stanford picked up the landline in his post and said, "There's someone approaching sector four. Request ART One to check it out." ART 1 sped to sector four and low and behold, it was Flight Sergeant Meeks.

The next afternoon at guardmount, Flight Sergeant Meeks said, "I didn't even get a chance to touch the fence. And because of that, Airman Stanford gets a day off."

Stanford completed his six year commitment. He graduated from Texas State University with a degree in criminal justice. He was hired by the FBI in 1998.

Investigator Mel Unger worked his life off as a sheriff under Broward County. He had his difficulties. First of all, he didn't have a degree. Second, his father was the Chief of Police. Third, the community was stale; they didn't care. Night after night, the only thing he heard was ASAP.

He once said, "If ya gonna cross Jesus, bring some wine."

In spite of that, Mel was honorable, dependable, and consistent. His greatest handicap? He was prejudice. Mel was Irish, which meant he was raised by people who were enslave, starved, and shunned. Affiliated with the Catholic church wasn't even a ray of hope.

Mel said, "Screw it in. And if it doesn't hold, throw it out."

Agent Stanford and Investigator Mel had one thing in common; loyalty to the law profession.

******

Sonny Carinii was a lofty, jolly, carefree punk. The only thing that kept him going was money. Money kept him alive. Without it, he would be dead as a dinosaur.

Sonny's life started as a runner for Big Shot Charlie. Big Shot gave him a start by collecting from businesses. It wasn't long before Sonny got overwhelmed. So, he hired two punks; Bartolome and Gin Gordon. They have been working for him until one of them ended up dead; Bartolome known as Crook.

Sonny's legacy was a saying, "Payback is the way back!" He worked on that one principle.

******

Gin German was an evil hood. That's all he knew. He would kill you, jack your car, and leave you on the side of the road to die.

Keith was different. He walked around with composer. He rarely got excited, but when he did.

"I'll break ya in two," he warned.

Now Jitterbug had a career in the entertainment industry. His day of busting heads and extortion were long gone. But what he liked, he liked to bust up Carinii's foot soldiers. Why? It happened one evening in Vegas.

Jitterbug had finished his set. He was at the blackjack table, and it appeared he was cleaning them out. From the casino point of view, they have to pay them for his set and, pay him for his wins. That would make it a bad night for the casino. What did the casino do? They hit the fire alarm.

People scattered. At the same time Jitterbug collected his chips. A security guard tried to stop him, but Jitterbug stiff-armed him and made his way out. The casino placed a letter at Jitterbug's suite the following day.

The letter said: Martin Sanders is no longer allowed in this casino.

Agent Stanford, Investigator Mel, Sonny, Keith, Gin German, and Jitterbug had one name in their pocket, Julius Wilbur.

Chapter 14

Nervous?

Marge shook Cheryl in bed. Friday morning was forecast to be hectic in her business. Bonnie Tyler's *Total Eclipse of the Heart* played on the radio as Marge got up and headed for the master bathroom. Marge's buttock jiggled as she turned toward the toilet. Cheryl kicked the cover off of her but remained naked in bed.

Marge said, "Come on lazy head, we got to get going. Don't wanna waste any time."

"I'm with you, but I need another go round to get going." She rolled on the bed and looked at the opened bathroom door.

Marge was naked when she said, "I hear you talking, but my ass isn't gonna get us paid." She walked out of the bathroom. To Cheryl, Marge's shape was exceedingly alluring.

Cheryl got up, and as Marge passed her, she palmed Marge's waxed genital. At the same time, Marge slapped Cheryl's ass. Cheryl strolled to the bathroom. When she walked in, she said, "What did you eat last night. Damn, it smells like spoiled fish."

"But you ate a lot of it last night," said Marge, "Hurry up. We gotta get going."

******

A knock on the door. Mel said, "Yeah, yeah, yeah, I'm coming." He got up, unlocked the door, and retreated to his bed.

Agent Stanford walked into the room. He said, "Ya'll hillbillies lay in bed too much. I'm ready to go to work."

Mel said, "Ready to go to work? What about the serial killer? His butt is getting a good night rest. While we're up looking under some woman's skirt."

"We need to go to Julius' apartment to see if he's home," said Stanford.

"Why do we need to do that?"

Stanford said, "If he's not home, there's a possibility he left town."

"Alright, alright," said Mel, "Let me get dressed."

******

Jay woke up, took a shower, and got dressed. He grabbed his car keys and left his apartment. After what Jitterbug had told him about Crook. It would be easy to convict him. As far as Jay was concerned, Crook was alive the last time people saw them together.

Jay drove to the pastry stand. The owner said, "Why did you do it?"

"Do what?"

"How could you kill Crook?"

Jay said, "Just give me that donut."

The owner wrapped the donut, handed it to Jay, and said, "Here."

Jay said, "Thanks." He got into his car and drove off.

Jay stopped at the news stand and got a newspaper.

The owner said, "It's not in there."

"What's not in there?" Jay asked.

"The article that you killed Crook," said the owner.

Jay paid for the newspaper, got into his car, and sped off.

******

Penny hustled. The Eagles' *I Can't Tell You Why* played on her radio. She tripped over her shoes, scrambled to gather her items, and then soared to the door. In next to no time, she was on the road. She thought of Jay's way of caring for women, but there was no time for that. Penny had placed him in the back of her mind and sped to her destination.

Sam woke up on the grumpy side. "Those hoes don't respect nothing but money," he thought. He got dressed and headed for the arena.

Pat had finished sharpening his clippers. At the last minute, he grabbed a chart to let Penny know this is the styles she choose. He packed them in a bag and made his way to the arena.

Janice was at peace. She has done all she could to make the show a success. She stood in front of a mirror and marveled at her physique. "They can't turn this down," she thought.

******

The expressways were jammed. Everyone wanted to arrive at the same place at the same time. Old Dell unlocked the loading door to Reese's Deep Seafood and stuck the key into his pocket.

Trucks were parked outside. Dell walked to the first truck and looked in the bed.

The driver said, "Fresh halibut, snow crabs, and king crabs from the Bering Strait of Alaska. Only refrigerated overnight."

Dell signed the receipt and said, "Over there,"

Dell examined the fish in the next truck, and then signed the receipt. He walked to the next truck. The bed was full of Maine lobsters in all sizes. He signed the receipt and moved to the next truck. The bed was full of shrimp from the Gulf of Mexico. He signed the receipt. And then there were twelve boxes of scallops already cleaned and cut.

Dell said, "Unload them over there." He pointed.

Inside Reese's it was warm. Cooks were heating oil and oven were getting warm.

******

Jitterbug laid in bed and thought of Cookie. She was carefree, firm, and if she had a man, he couldn't hold her down. Cookie knew how to work it in bed. That gal could go.

"How did I miss out on that?" He thought.

He got up, got dressed, and then hit the streets.

******

A carpenter pounded the last nail. The set was erected. The carpenters had worked through the night building the most spectacular background and catwalk.

The supervisor said as he looked at the stage, "We'll have to wait here until Miss Gray arrive. Once we get her approval, you can leave."

A minute later, Marge and Cheryl walked into the arena. Marge gasp when she understood something clearly at last reflected from the stage. In the middle at the back of the stage was a soaring lighthouse. The walls were pearl white and surrounded the lighthouse. The catwalk had an ocean turquoise tint. The seating was arranged circularly in an attempt to include the audience in the show. Several air tanks were set off to the side.

Marge walked up to the supervisor and said, "You broke your foot off in this. It's magnificent."

"You like it," he said.

Cheryl said, "Like it? We love it!"

The supervisor said, "Glad you like it. We're going to run the salted sea air tanks behind the stage." He pointed and shouted, "Move those tanks behind the stage." The workers went to work. He handed her a tablet and said, "Sign here."

Marge handed the tablet back to the supervisor and said to Cheryl, "Let's go to the dressing room. We're going to make sure it's ready to receive."

• •

******

James Earl drove the truck to Alton Arena. He backed into the loading dock and said to his assistant, "Let's off load these clothes and get the hell out of here."

They felt a bump when he hit the dock. They got out and opened the back doors.

The assistant said, "Let's get to work."

"If you move your lazy ass, we can get something done," said James Earl.

Marge came out of the door that leads to the loading dock. She said, "You're on time. Let's make sure we got everything." She held a clipboard and began to check off items.

Penny turned her radio on and began to stir sugar in her tea. When the weather report ended, Lenny William's *Suspicion* played. She couldn't shake her downhearted feeling. She wondered, "Why would Jay lie to me?"

******

Two weeks ago, Marge said, "We're in the middle of production and we don't have a solid finance."

Penny said, "Might be able to get it." She picked up a Financial Times magazine, flip through the pages, pointed, and said, "Here's, King, and Associates. It says," she mumbled and then continued, "Venues, big event productions, and other exhibits."

Marge said, "Give them a call. Let me know what they say."

Jay was at his Atlanta home in his pool. His phone rang. He got out of the pool and answered, "King and Associates."

"Hello, this is Penny Clark of Angel Inc. Is this the right number for financing?"

Jay said, "No, it's not, but I can get you the correct number. Hold on."

Penny listened carefully. She heard him walk back to the phone. Jay said, "The number is 404…"

"Thank you," said Penny.

He said, "I'm going to be in your city Friday. Perhaps I can save you some time and meet with you about financing your event."

"That'll be great," said Penny. "See you Friday. Give me a call and I'll pick you up at the airport. My number is 678…"

Friday came and Penny was at the airport. Passenger began to flow through the doors. A handsome man stood tall and erect. He search the waiting vehicles as though he was expecting a ride.

"I bet that's him," Penny wondered. She opened her door and yelled from her car, "Julius Wilbur?"

His attention was at once drawn to her. He hustled and got into her Mercedes.

She said, "I'm Penny Clark, welcome."

"I'm Julius Wilbur. Good to meet you. I need you to take me to Albany Transportation to pick up my car."

She said, "Why are you here?"

"I have to drop off some funds. After I do that, we can talk about your business venture."

She said, "How long will it take?"

"We should wrap the deal up tomorrow," said Jay as he continued, "I'll sponsor twenty-five thousand and front my company one million. Piece of cake. I'll be here in a couple of weeks to see how things are going. I also have to check on this investment."

That should have been a red flag. Why is he coming back to check his investments? Penny didn't care. She yearned to see him again. It turned out, he's a murderer. She decided to let him, "Love me to death."

******

Cee Note said to Will, "When she see this ring, she's gonna flip out."

Will said, "Don't know why you wanna get married. You can get any babe you want. But that's just me."

Cee Note said, "What you have against Leola?"

"Don't think she's into you," said Will, "Is that a crime? Boss you're going into strange territory. I say let it be."

Cee Note said, "I'm gonna marry her. Either you agree or I'll find another advisor."

"I'll send you a postcard," said Will, "And by the way, I think she's sweet on Julius Wilbur. And you're telling me, you didn't peep that?"

"Why rain on my parade when you can piss on it," said Cee Note, "Success to you is like a slap in the face. Get over it. It's gonna happen."

Will responded, "Over my dead body," as he walked out of the den.

******

"Is that the best you can do?" Jay asked over the phone.

The caller said, "That's it."

Jay hung up. Jay realized he was in deep water with the law. Most people knew he was a killer. Mickey's murder left him exposed. No one would come within a mile of him. How do you counteract that? You go to the source.

******

Sam Lovely scolded, "Nicki pull that dress out the crack of your butt. The site of that is enough to make King David limp."

Sam Lovely arrived early to check the measurements of the costumes. He had Nicki come in early because of her unique figure. Next was Cira.

Cira asked, "How does this look?"

"Like a gospel choir without a church," answered Sam. "The look has to be lovely, firm, and with a kick you in your butt look."

An assistant walked up to him and said, "Leola is here."

"Hurry, send her in."

Leola sauntered into the dressing room.

Sam said, "Try this on." He handed her a skirt.

Sam said as she fastened the skirt, "Laud have mercy. That must be jelly because jam don't wiggle like that."

Leola said, "Is that all you got to say?"

Sam said, "Naw, I'll smash that and I'm gay!"

The assistant said, "Cookie is here."

Cookie walked up to him and said, "Don't need any sizing. I need a man." She said wagging her head.

"There're many men under that bridge," said Sam, "Your butt needs to concentrate on this show and that costume needs to be adjusted. Ya dig?"

Cookie put on a dress and a seamstress made the adjustments.

******

A repeating knock at the door. Jay opened it. Agent Stanford and Investigator Mel barged in.

Agent Stanford asked, "Where were you at about eleven last night?"

"I left to see a lady friend, and then I came back here."

Mel said, "You're a lying piece of crap. You shot Barry Johnson.

Stanford waved his hand and said, "Why is it that you always have an alibi? Mel thinks you killed Barry Johnson and all you say is, you were somewhere else?"

"All I can do is tell you the truth," said Jay, "All you do is keep accusing me. You have my attorney's name and contact number. I suggest you contact them for any further questions." Jay turned from them and said, "Now, I got to get going. You have a have a wonderful day."

Mel said, "We're going to that fashion show tonight with our eyes on you. So, we will have a wonderful night when we bust ya." He and Stanford left.

Jay closed the door.

******

Eddie Grant arrived at the arena for fitting. Sam yelled, "It's about time. You're on colored people time, but the world is on time. But you're gorgeous and you know it," said Sam as he looked Eddie's body over.

Eddie said, "Ain't got all day. And if you touch my…"

"You're not that gorgeous," Sam interrupted and continued, "Hold up your arms." He took measurements and said, "I need you to come in early this afternoon so we can make sure things look good."

Eddie nodded.

Chapter 15

Anyhow, Any Way

It was early afternoon Friday when Jitterbug walked into Jasper's, a restaurant on the lower east side. He sat at a table across from Sonny.

Sonny said, "Are ya gonna do it?"

"Is Macy's opened?" Asked Jitterbug as he continued, "Yeah, I'm gonna do it."

Sonny said, "Well, I hope you do it. I'll be there just in case you change your mind."

Jitterbug said, "I'll be there. You just make sure my ride is waiting." Jitterbug assumed Sonny had planned his murder. So, he will have a ride waiting because no one walks away from a hit like this.

"Of course, a car will be waiting," said Sonny, "Ya think I'm an amateur?"

Leola strutted from her uptown condo with flair. She thought of how she was going to trap Julius. Leola knew Jay didn't stand a chance against her ending up immensely wealthy after tonight. Cookie had no chance at him; Marge was too old and gay for him. Cheryl only liked women, and Penny was too prim for him. She thought as she looked into a mirror, "When I throw this on him, he'll be mine."

******

A knock at the door. Jay opened it and Penny walked in. She was dressed in a black evening gown. He was dressed in a white tuxedo jacket with black bowtie, coma bond, and pants. He strolled back to a piano he had bought and began to play it in the dark. He knew he wasn't going to live through the night and that he wasn't going to gaze upon her face again. Jay was satisfied. He had a good life.

She said, "Ready?"

"No, but no man is ready for death," said Jay, "Investigators came this morning and told me they knew I killed Mickey and Crook. They're going to arrest me at the show, but I've got to hold on." He looked at her and said, "I love you."

She turned from him in an attempt to ease the pain and said, "Let's go."

Her eyes were soggy as she conquered traffic.

******

Models and staff began to arrive at the arena. Nicki said, "Where's my skirt?"

Cira said, "It's on the table over there. Lose some weight."

Nicki said, "My butt bring dollars. What do your butt bring?"

"A lively hood," said Cira.

Pat said, "Ladies remove your scarves and let's get ready to rumble."

Sam said, "Don't look like a hoochy mama. Strut with grace and style."

Warren examined each hair style. He said, "Pat, touch this up."

Pat moved to Cira. Warren said, "Sam, is she pregnant?"

Sam said, "Hell no, what you're talking about?"

Warren said, "Look at that belly."

"That's for pregnant women, you dope."

Warren looked at Cookie's hair and said, "If I wasn't gay, I'll bang ya in a minute."

Leola was relaxed in her chair. Her tan thighs kept Pat peeping at her legs as he worked on Nicki's hair.

Leola said, "I need a real man."

Sam said, "Me too."

Warren said, "Anything would do."

Leola's heart craved Jay. She was determined to make it happened.

At the same time, Eddie passed Frank as he stood close to the door. Eddie said, "You look familiar."

Frank said, "I've never been to one of your gay parties. So, you didn't see me there. I date Cookie. She's over there." He pointed at her.

Eddie said, "Maybe that's where I've seen you. By the way, I'm not gay."

******

Penny and Jay arrived at the arena. She parked in an employee slot, they got out, and went inside. Jay walked to his seat. Agent Stanford and Investigator Mel walked over to him.

Stanford said, "We're over there." He pointed at their seats.

Mel said, "Four eyes are on you. So don't try to run."

Jay looked up to them and said, "And you call yourselves cops. Why not arrest me now? You can't. Circumstance evidence is a Hail Mary in the legal system. The prosecutors pray the jury catches it." He returned his attention to his bulletin.

Stanford said, "We're waiting for more evidence. And since you're so sloppy, we're get it before the show is over." They went to their seats.

******

Limousines pulled to the entrance of the arena. Fashionably dressed women and men got out and strolled passed Jitterbug. He was waiting outside the arena main door when Sonny Carinii walked up.

Sonny said, "I'll wait at the other end of the arena. In case he comes out on that side."

Jitterbug nodded and said, "Got it."

******

By now, people began to arrive and stroll into the arena. Acquaintances met, embraced, and chat before taking their seats. Other attendees took their seats and studied their bulletins. Jay visually searched them.

Stanford and Mel followed Jay eyes.

Mel said, "Who is he looking for?"

"Probably his next victim."

Mel said, "What do you mean?"

"He's here to kill someone."

Mel said, "Kill who?"

"Don't know, but if we follow the money trail," said Stanford, "he'll be tied to it."

******

Marge peeked the audience from backstage. She turned to Cheryl and said, "They're coming. It's going to be a pretty big crowd. I didn't realize they would accept my Haute couture creations."

Cheryl said, "You're famous. What did you expect?"

"I didn't expect they loved my style this much."

Cheryl looked at her and said, "Why do you think I hang around. Don't know what I'll do if something happened to you."

"Don't worry," said Marge, "Nothing going to happen to me." She looked away and shouted, "Janice!"

* * * * * *

Reese's Catering arrived to offload their cargo. Packaged precooked seafood and condiments were taken to a section of the arena set aside for the after party. The guest tables name plates were placed in such a way, commonality was assured. The manager of Reese's Catering crew directed how the tables would be dressed.

He said, "Cover each table with the white tablecloth. And then place a knife, fork, and spoon per person for four on each table." He paused and continued, "Bring the food in here to heat it up. When the food is brought out, we'll place a seafood plater and condiments on each table." He pointed at the bartender and ordered, "Marshal, setup and mind the bar."

* * * * * *

Jay looked at Stanford and Mel. Stanford and Mel looked at him. The arena was getting pretty crowded. Outside, Sonny and Jitterbug was getting a little worried. How could they conduct their operation with so many people? Jitterbug thought, "Screw this," and walked away.

On the other hand, and on the other side, Sonny waited. Killing a man never bothered him. That was in his job description; mobster. If he carried this job out, it would seal his ambition of becoming an underboss.

* * * * * *

Barbara Mason's *Another Man* played over the speakers. Marge walked around to thank the people for coming to her show. She walked up to Jay and said, "See, I told you so."

Jay smiled and said, "A good investment is a good investment."

She looked at him and said, "What do you think about homosexuals?"

"I never think about them," said Jay.

Marge said, "We had a problem with finance until you came along. I believe you're being harass because of it."

"Is it because homosexuality is an abomination to God or is it our take on sexuality," said Jay, "If God wanted us to get rid of gay people, he could've had Lot do it. But he didn't, and gay people still exist. So, there must be another reason for Sodom and Gomorrah. Until I find out what that reason is, I'm going to go mind my own business instead of going around trying to play God."

Marge smiled and said, "Interesting, thanks," she moved on to greet another patron.

******

Jitterbug went to Maggie's and sat down at the counter.

The server said, "You're Martin Sanders that singer. How's it going?"

He said, "I must be out of my mind. Why am I doing jobs for the Carinii syndicate when I have a singing career?"

She said, "Coming to your senses is a mother. Don't throw your life away for those dead beats."

"They're not dead beats," said Jitterbug, "They're human beings trying to make a living. Everyone ain't rich."

She said, "What do you want? A meal or a handkerchief?"

******

The attendees were seated. The lights began to dim with the exception of the catwalk light. It remained bright. The air began to smell of sea salt as though they were on a beach. Fleetwood Mac's introduction to *Everywhere* began to play. Cookie strutted from backstage into the light of the catwalk.

Eric Neat, the comedic host said, "For Marge Gray's bedroom attire set. Cookie is wearing an empire line shear teddy with matching shear panties."

Cookie strutted to the end, posed, and pivot. She strutted back down the catwalk and passed Cira as she strutted up in a pink babydoll silhouette.

When Cira pivot and strutted back down the catwalk, she passed Nicki in a loose fitting green pajama set. Nicki pivoted and then strutted back down the catwalk.

When Leola appeared in a negligee, Eric said, "Hot damn."

She strutted, in high heels, passed Nicki. When she reached the end of the catwalk, she paused, pivot, and seductively swung her hip at Jay. And then she marched back down the catwalk."

Eric wiped sweat and said, "Now for men attire."

The men appeared one by one, but Marge kept Eddie for last. She said to him, "Loose the pajama top and slippers."

Eddie took off the pajama top and flipped his slippers off.

She said, "Now strut."

When Eddie walked into the light of the catwalk, "Oh and ah," came from the audience. The pajama bottoms hit at the lower stomach just above the lumbar. He walked so seductively that a lady fainted in the audience. He paused, pivot, and then strutted back down the catwalk.

Olivia Newton John's *Physical* played for the next set, athletics. Cookie walked into the light in a black tee and black tights. She paused, pivot, and strutted passed Cira in a bathing suit. Cira paused, pivot, and strutted passed Nicki in a sweatshirt, sweatpants, and sneakers. Nicki paused, pivot, and walked back down the catwalk.

Leola walked into the light in a skimpy black bikini and black six inch heels. She strutted on the catwalk with her hips swaying from side to side. She stopped, paused, pivot, and look directly into Jay's eyes. She turned and walked back down the catwalk.

Eric proclaimed, "Jesus sweat," as he wiped sweat. "Now for the men."

Backstage, Marge said to Eddie who was wearing Speedos, "Be mindful, your junk might slip out. If it does, play it off. Make lemonade. Now go."

When Eddie stepped into the light, women screamed for his pleasure. He walked to the end of the catwalk, paused, but when he pivot, his junk flopped out. Women skreiched louder. He tucked it back in and walked back down the catwalk as if nothing had happened.

Eric Neat said, "Holy cow, he's so big, he needs a forklift to take a leak. Now for the casual attire set."

Hot Chocolate's introduction to *Everyone a Winner* repeatedly played. Cookie hit the catwalk in a yellow knife pleat mini skirt, a mock white halter, and yellow pumps. She passed Cira in Daisey Dukes denim, a red bikini top, with platform sandals. Cira passed Nicki in a purple tee, worn and torn jeans, with white Chuck Taylors Converse. She made it backstage when Leola hit the catwalk light in a white see through dress with white sandals. She strutted to the end of the catwalk, struck a pose, walked to Jay, and beguilingly threw her hips towards him. She strutted back down the catwalk.

Eric said as he looked backstage, "Get my heart medicine. That Leola is gonna be the death of me."

Eddie walked down the catwalk in a white u-tee shirt, white beach pants, and sandals. Some of the women shook their heads out of cynicism.

One lady shouted, "He's finer than a fine-tooth comb."

When Eddie left the catwalk, Eric said, "Now for our final set, evening attire."

The male models went first. They made their way back down the catwalk and stood on one side of backstage. After Eddie modeled in a black tuxedo with jetted pockets, the music started.

Cee Note sang as he walked onto the catwalk. His high impact, throbbing bass song *High Tonight* hit number one on billboards chart last week.

He strolled to the side of the catwalk and sang, "Gonna be great tonight, that's what I'm gonna do. Gonna get high tonight because I'm with you."

The lead guitarist improvised in a raging way. The bass guitarist roved the bass. The keyboard and synthesizer player improvised a stinging melody. The drummer stroke the drums in such a way, it was nearly impossible to lose the rhythm. Cee Note sang on.

Cookie pranced into the light in a yellow X-line silhouette dress with yellow heels. She paused at the end of the catwalk, pivot, and then strutted back down the catwalk. She passed Cira in a strapless black dress with a long vent silhouette in the front.

Cira did her thing and passed Nicki in a white spaghetti strap evening gown. Nicki made it back down the catwalk as Leola in a shear, eggshell gown with visible black bra and tong panties entered the light.

Stanford said to Mel, "We'll take him after she leaves the stage. And remember he's weak in his left peripheral vision. So, it's important, we approach him from his left."

"Gotcha, Stan," said Mel.

Leola strutted up the catwalk to the end. She paused. At the other end of the catwalk Cee Note kneeled to one knee. The munition supervisor flipped the switch. An explosion occur that left everything hidden in smoke except Leola. She pivoted, winked at Jay, turned, and walked back down the catwalk.

The smoke started to disperse from the catwalk. When Leola reached Cee Note, she screamed, "Oh my God," and looked for Jay. He wasn't in his seat.

Stanford and Mel looked to the catwalk and saw Cee Note lying flat on his back with a ring case in his hand. They looked toward Jay, and he wasn't in his seat. They searched the scattering mob and saw Jay shoving and pushing his way through them for the entrance.

Outside, people scrambled in panic from the arena. Sonny saw Jay run out of the arena and duck into an alley. He ran after him.

Jay ran down the alley but didn't notice a dumpster on his left. He ran passed it and heard a click.

"You're about as dumb as a rock," said Frank with a pistol pointed at him.

Jay turned around and slowly raised his hands.

By this time, Stanford and Mel arrived in the alley. Stanford motioned Mel to be quiet. Stanford and Mel listened.

Sonny stopped at the beginning of the alley and listened.

Frank said, "You're right. I killed Cee Note, but you'll get blamed for it. And guess what, I killed Mickey King because he sent you here to kill me. I killed Crook because he was supposed to kill you. So, I did you a favor, but I knew he was your strength. I got your money and I'm gonna keep it. Anyway, you're not gonna need it where you're going."

Jay said with composure, "So, you're the charlatan."

"And you're a charlatan, pretending you're a murderer. So long, Jay Dub."

The crowd coming out of the arena saw four flashes in the alley, and then heard four reports.

Jay patted his torso. He wasn't hit. Sonny hit Frank in the back with a shot. Frank spun around and fired. Sonny hit Frank with a headshot. Mel fired his pistol and wounded Sonny. Sonny tumbled to the pavement.

Stanford rushed over to searched Frank, pulled his wallet, and said, "Frances Ross."

Mel said, "His name appeared on one of the manifest last Wednesday in Florida."

People stood at the entrance to the alley. An ambulance arrived and medical personnel began to muscle their way through spectators. Among the spectators was Eddie. He looked at Frank's body and said to Penny, "I knew I had seen him before. I went to Joey Donte's, and I saw him sitting in a car across the street. When I came out of the store, I saw him get out of the car and gun down Piru. Now, he's dating Cookie who was Piru's lady. It makes sense, he killed Piru to get Cookie."

Jay said to Stanford, "Your suspicion was drawn to me, the wrong guy. He's the one you're looking for." He pointed at Frank.

Mel said, "It was me who was wrong. Should have known better. However, you're not who you pretend to be either. You're not a gangster. You can go. Go on, get outta here."

Jay went back to the arena. He searched the dressing room and found Penny sitting in a chair weeping as paramedics lugged Cee Notes' body bag onto a gurney. Security scrambled all over the arena.

Jay walked up to Penny and said, "I apologize, but I didn't want you to get involved." She stood and he held her in his arms.

"Eddie told me Frank killed Piru," said Penny, "I was wrong about you. You're not a murderer."

Marge told security guards, "Help yourself to the seafood. She turned and said to Cheryl, "We got ambushed by a murderer. I saw what he saw," she pointed at Jay. "We saw Frank shoot Cee Note."

Jay said to Penny, "Let's leave this place and go to mine."

******

Leola's limousine parked in front of a hangar at the airport. Her Lear jet was pulled out to the taxiway and its engines purred. She climbed aboard and said, "He killed Cee Note for me."

Her agent said, "He didn't kill him. I saw him in his seat when the explosion happened."

"Well, who killed him," asked Leola.

Her agent said, "It was Cookie's man."

"That hoe," said Leola, "She was jealous of me. We'll wait for Jay Dub."

Her agent said with reluctance, "He's not coming," she said, "I saw him with Penny Clark."

Leola shouted to the pilot, "Let's go!"

******

Jitterbug arrived at the arena. The surroundings were hectic. Police shouted and cursed, women sobbing, and security guards searched for a reason how this could happen. He walked into the dressing room. He smiled at Cookie; she smiled back.

She said, "Let's blow this place," and they left.

******

Now, Eddie was on the short end of the whole incident. He was left with no one to love. Conversely, that wasn't an issue. His issue was, will he get another gig?

Marge walked up to him, hugged him, and kissed him on his cheek. She said, "It wasn't your fault. The audience loved you. So, you'll always have a gig with me."

"Didn't know women would react to me like that," said Eddie, "How can I get work around here?"

Marge said, "You'll get work. That's no problem. Your problem is turning down gigs."

He smiled at her.

******

Penny and Jay laid in bed. Dexter Wansel's *Together Once Again* began to play. He got up, went into the kitchen, and returned. After he crawled under the sheets, he said, "I'm going to close my lease and leave tomorrow. My work is done here."

The Platters' Great Pretender began to play.

Penny said, "Do you have to go?"

"Yes, I do, and I want you to come with me." On an audio system played, *"Pretending you're still around,"* Tony Willams slowed the song tempo. "*You're still around,*" Zola Taylor and the rest of The Platters brought the song to an end.

- 129 -

The End

Other Novels by David L. Simmons
The Last Matriarch: Day of the Robin
The Last Matriarch: Bob White
The Fishbowl
GIP
Ammon's Curse

www.ingramcontent.com/pod-product-compliance
Lightning Source LLC
Chambersburg PA
CBHW021326060726
47591CB00006B/1887